Lord Justin's face sobered. "My very dear, it will not do, you know."

"You mean because I am an insipid miss? Pola had been in love with many men and knew how to please you in that way. Well, I am sure that in London I could very soon come by tuition in that, as easily as in whist or piquet!"

In an instant Milord had seized her so tightly in his arms that she could hardly breathe. "If ever I hear you make such an outrageous suggestion again..."

"If you must have an experienced partner, and I am supremely ignorant, and you reject the idea of another man instructing me, then you, it seems, must be my teacher."

"The idea is not without its charm," admitted Milord, kissing the tip of her nose.

Fawcett Crest Books
by Elizabeth Chater:

ELIZABETH CHATER

MILADY HOT-AT-HAND

FAWCETT CREST • NEW YORK

For a gallant lady—Elizabeth Patricia

A Fawcett Crest Book
Published by Ballantine Books
Copyright © 1981 by Elizabeth Chater

ISBN 0-449-21176-2

Manufactured in the United States of America

First Fawcett Crest Edition: February 1981
First Ballantine Books Edition: November 1986

Chapter One

ANDREA HAD BEEN IN LONDON only two days when she was made aware that some threat challenged her father's peace of mind. It had been so exciting to be summoned from her school in Switzerland, brought to England under the chaperonage of Cousin Stacia, and established in a great mansion in London, reunited once again with the father and sister who, aside from Stacia, were all the family she had in the world. Her recurring hope that *this time* things would be different, this time father would make an effort to be with her, that Pola would share the fun of being a girl, had soon been disappointed. Things were as they had always been. The handsome, ageing Count Vladimir Wasylyk was his urbane charming self, as always more interested in his social life and in gaming with his cronies than in a daughter he scarcely ever saw.

Pola had become more waspish than ever. She was such a flamboyant beauty with her dark-red hair and green eyes that it was no wonder she was constantly besieged by men and too busy to bother with an awkward young half sister. Cousin Stacia had confided, during the journey to England, that Pola had pulled off the coup of the season. She had captured the prize in the matrimonial stakes, Lord Dominic Justin of Kyle in Scotland, of whom all the hopeful mamas had long despaired. This was indeed a triumph, advised Stacia, since Milord had estates not only in Scotland and England, but in France and Spain as well, his forebears having consistently married heiresses whose beauty was exceeded only by their wealth.

"He is too starched up for my taste," Stacia confided, "but la! child, his family is older than the current royalty's!"

Stacia had prattled on, "I must confess to you, my love, that I have been more than a little concerned over your sister. Pola is a strikingly beautiful woman, but she is—wayward." Stacia primmed her lips. "Of course you don't know what I'm talking about! How should you, child, having been banished to that dreary seminary in Geneva—such a dull place, in spite of the excellence of its teachers! I daresay you can speak more than one language, and even cipher?"

In spite of her interest in Stacia's original subject, Andrea had to smile as she answered, "Oh, yes indeed, Cousin! I've been well taught: philosophy, history, mathematics, composition and grammar, as well as an unimpeachable accent in French and English—"

"Say no more, I implore you!" cried her cousin. "I beg of you, Andrea, *never* let this be known in London, where even the half of your scholarly accomplishments would insure your remaining a spinster all your days! What was Vladi thinking of, to send you to such a hive of bluestockings?"

"He was thinking of getting me out from underfoot," said Andrea sadly. "You know he is too busy to bother with a gangling girl-child."

Cousin Stacia was not betrayed into maudlin pity. " 'Tis your own blame! You've done your best to be a son to him whenever he has let you come home to Poland," she said roundly. "I warn you, Andrea, my love, you'll get nowhere with Vladi unless you employ feminine wiles. Force him to acknowledge you as a woman—charm him as Pola does! No more of this hoydenish fencing and riding your horses astride over the roughest terrain!" She gave an elaborate shudder.

Andrea thought of the long-awaited vacations every year, when she could come home to the palace in Warsaw in the winter and to Castle Wasylyk in the summer vacation. She loved that dark, brooding, uncomfortable place with a deep love which only her father shared. It was one of the few bonds she had with him, and she tried to strengthen it every chance she got. In those vast, echoing stone halls beneath the painted stare of long-dead ancestors, Count Vladimir had taught her to fence. Also he had taken her hawking with him, and together they had galloped across the mountain meadows and along the craggy heights where only the wild rams kept them company. At such times Andrea felt she was truly her father's daughter.

Yet even here Pola had come between them. She could ride better than most men, and she often accompanied them on their day-long rides into the hills. When Andrea had been banished to her room before dinner, Pola, who was nine years older, was allowed to join her father and his guests at the table. There, beautifully gowned and voluptuously lovely, she kept the guests—at least the masculine ones—in a pleasant state of awareness of her desirability. Andrea had often watched from the upper hallway as Pola swept down the great staircase below her, jewels sparkling in the light of a thousand candles.

Her nurse had caught her there one night.

"It isn't fair, Nonna!" the child had wept. "I am never let to go down! It is always Pola who has the fun!"

Nonna had muttered darkly as she led the child back to her bedroom. "I do not know what your father can be thinking of," she was talking more to herself than to the child. "He's amused by that wicked girl. She delights in rousing men to a passion and then laughing at them! One day she'll meet a real man, not one of these mincing fops, and then Milady Pola will get her comeuppance, mark my words!" She put Andrea back to bed with rough tenderness, then sighed. "It's because she's the image of her mother that he can't deny her anything. It is too bad you—" then Nonna broke off infuriatingly, and told

Andrea quite crossly to get to sleep at once, or it would be the worse for her.

Fuming, the girl wondered how anyone could get to sleep in the face of such a provocative statement, and resolved to ask her father why it was too bad she didn't look like her mother.

Two days later, after a bout of fencing in which Andrea's growing skill had pleased Count Vladimir, she asked him why she didn't resemble her mother.

"But you do, my poppet," he assured her. "Thick golden hair and those unusual amber eyes. Although I think you have something of my features—a handsome blending, I would say. When you're grown you may even be a beauty."

"As beautiful as Pola?" ventured the girl.

Vladimir hesitated. "No one could be as beautiful as Pola," he said at length. "She is the image of her mother, my first wife." Thus Andrea learned that her father had had two wives, of whom her own was the less attractive, since Pola's mother still held all his love.

Unwisely, she sought further information from Pola.

"Of course we had different mothers," the older girl sneered. "Mine was papa's first choice, a dazzling Russian aristocrat who looked just as I do, and had so much fire and daring that she was a fitting bride for The Wasylyk. You know our family motto: *Toujours l'audace!* Always bold! We never refuse a challenge. That's how she came to die," said Pola. "She wanted to ride a new horse one of her admirers had given her. Papa refused to let her—it was a fiery unbroken beast, and anyway he resented her accepting such a gift from a man he didn't particularly like. But mama would never be told what to do, any more than I will," she interpolated fiercely. "So she had the animal saddled and bridled and rode off over the mountain trails." Her expression darkened. "They found her body crushed under the horse at the foot of the cliff."

Andrea couldn't find words to express her compassion. She moved closer to her sister and laid a gentle hand over hers. Pola threw it off disdainfully.

"And that's why, four years later, to recoup the family fortunes, papa married your mother, who was, did you know? not at all noble but a mine-owner's daughter and so rich that even Count Vladi will never be able to spend the half of it!" She glanced spitefully at the child. "Your mama died in birthing *you* instead of the son papa had hoped for. So you see—"

But Andrea had run from the room, wounded more deeply than even she realized by Pola's malice.

At the end of that disastrous summer, Andrea was sent to a select academy in Switzerland, to be taught the graces and the conduct which would be required of her as Count Wasylyk's daughter. Incidentally she received the excellent education for which the school was renowned throughout Europe. Although she was allowed to spend her brief school holidays with her father, there was never again the feeling of family, nor was she able to convince herself that she mattered personally to anyone, except perhaps Stacia. This lady, widow of a distant cousin, had been installed as official chaperone for Pola, who ignored her when she was not defying her. Cousin Stacia was the only person who ever gave Andrea a feeling of belonging, so it was with real pleasure that the girl embarked with her upon the exciting trip to London.

But from what Stacia was saying now, things would be no different, no better than they had been. "Why did he send for me, Stacia?" she asked wistfully.

"You are to be a bridesmaid—the only one," she added grimly. "Pola has made no friends among the other girls of good family. For one thing, she's too old for the debutante group— she's twenty-six, and practically an ape-leader, for all her flirtatious ways. Never found anyone she could settle on. Just like your father—but there," Stacia caught herself up, "I mustn't fret you with my silly gabble-mongering." It was hard, the older woman thought, to remember that this grave, amber-eyed girl was only seventeen and a virtual infant as far as worldly knowledge went. Her serious, interested manner invited one to run on, to confide matters which had better not be spoken of, and surely not before such a child. Smiling, she patted the slender hand on the seat beside her. "Not much further now, my dear. We'll be in your father's new home within the hour."

Andrea looked out the window, but she saw nothing of the country they were driving through. Instead she wondered about the haste with which she had been summoned to take part in this wedding ceremony—and even more confusing, why it was taking place in London rather than in Count Vladimir's palace in Warsaw.

Two nights after her arrival in London, Andrea got the first inkling that there was some menace to her family in this very unusual wedding. She heard her father and Stacia discussing the guest list. Count Vladi firmly overruled Stacia's timid suggestion that they invite some old family friends from Poland.

"No, my dear cousin, you know we had agreed to keep the group small. Kyle himself doesn't want a splash—the poor devil's been avoiding Parson's mousetrap for years! He's little like to want to play off his consequence for the delectation of a mob of curious gapeseeds."

Stacia had bridled. "I find your English slang grossly offensive, Vladi! Where you pick up these canting expressions—! Still, you do not put me off. Uncle Ignace can scarcely be called a gapeseed, nor can Great Aunt Tylla!—whatever *is* a gapeseed?" she broke off to enquire.

Count Vladimir chuckled. "The kind of rural rustic who wishes to come to a wedding of people he doesn't care a fig for," he advised her. "You know those two dodderers haven't given any of us a thought for years—unless it was to shake their heads over our scandalous behavior."

Stacia had to admit that was true, but she held to her point. "There is something havey-cavey about this ceremony which disturbs me."

" 'Havey-cavey'? Now there's a fine English phrase for a nice Polish aristocrat to use," he teased her.

"You won't trick me into abandoning my subject," Stacia warned him. "What is behind this quiet, hurried ceremony?"

Vladimir seemed to be weary of the conversation. He rose and walked toward the door of Stacia's sitting room. Andrea, ensconced on a window seat outside the door in the hallway, drew back into a corner behind a drapery. She *must* hear what her father had to say in answer to Stacia's question. But all he said, in a cool, bored voice, was, "You had better ask Kyle. It's as much his pigeon as Pola's."

When he had strolled off, Andrea returned to her room. After dinner that evening she was summoned by a maid to Pola's bedroom to discuss her bridesmaid's dress. Approaching the door, she overheard her father's voice raised in anger. "I seem to be eavesdropping all the time now," the girl thought distressfully. But it was becoming increasingly important to her to discover what was behind the behavior of Count Vladi and Pola.

"—tell you she *is* family!" Vladi was saying angrily.

Pola's tone was icy. "Not quite. She is the mine-owner's grandchild."

"And my daughter!"

"You've got dozens of them in Poland, I dare swear—" began Pola with a sneer.

"You go too far." Count Vladimir's voice was as cold as his daughter's. "Andrea is my legal child. Her mother's fortune bought your new hunter and the emeralds, and is paying for your trousseau—"

"You evade the issue," Pola interrupted, her voice rising. "She should never have been brought here for her own sake. She was safer in that school. You read the note! Her life could be in danger in London!"

With a rare flash of venom, Count Vladi interrupted. "Or she might outshine you, my pet? She's grown into a striking girl. Not just every man's taste, perhaps—"

Pola's laughter made Andrea shrink.

"Not any man's taste while I am here, Vladi! The child is a boy-girl, graceless and without charm. Send her back to her safe, sexless halls of academe, papa! Maybe a professor will offer for her!"

Andrea crept back to her own bedroom. She would not answer when Pola's maid came to see why she had not gone to her sister's room to try on the bridesmaid's dress.

Chapter Two

IN THE NEXT TEN DAYS Andrea was swept into a whirl—if not the social round, at least a small back-eddy—of activity. It seemed she had nothing to wear which would not disgrace the family, even if no one was likely to see her. The days were busy with visits from dressmakers, bonnet-makers, coiffeuses, shoemakers, even a tailor for the new riding habit Vladi ordered for her, with a skirt so long and sweeping that it had to be draped over one arm. Andrea, jealous of the comfort of breeches, hated it.

There were *vendeuses* who brought frothy undergarments and scarves and veils, and one formidable female with a moustache who came to fit the bridesmaid's dress. Andrea saw little of Pola, who openly resented her presence in London. Unhappily, she saw even less of her father. She did not feel particularly neglected, since neither member of her family had ever had time for her. Still, her sense of anxiety fully roused by the remarks she had overheard, she ventured into her father's book-room two nights before the wedding. Count Vladi was, for once, alone. He was enjoying a glass of brandy and a cigar.

15

"Papa," she said quietly, "why are we here?"

The man frowned at her before he answered. "I should have thought it clearly evident," he made a humorous gesture toward her elaborate evening gown. "We are preparing for Pola's wedding."

Andrea persisted. "But why here, in England? Why not in Warsaw?"

"Do not puzzle your head with such matters, child," he began; then, sensitive for once to the expression on her face, he vouchsafed her a plausible explanation. "I made a better alliance for Pola here in England than I could have done at home," he said lightly. "Pity the poor father who has two daughters to marry off, and no son to secure the succession and the rents. I suppose I shall have to look about for a suitable *parti* for you before long," he concluded, and took a hearty mouthful of his brandy as though the prospect daunted him.

Although he conversed kindly enough with her for a few minutes longer, enquiring about the school and her activities there, he soon tired of the unaccustomed role of *pater familias,* and dismissed her to Cousin Stacia in the ladies' parlor.

In the pleasantly impersonal confines of this room, Andrea faced an inquisition from Stacia. "Whyever did you choose that gown, child? It's ages too old for you, and the color makes you look bilious."

"Pola chose it," said Andrea woodenly.

Stacia shot her a glance, and then changed the subject.

After an hour of desultory chit-chat, Andrea excused herself and escaped to her room and the novel she had borrowed from the lending library. But even that soporific failed, and Andrea was forced to consider her situation.

Her father and sister had left Poland and come to England. Pola had been launched most successfully into the beau monde, and had gratified all her well-wishers by securing a prize, Lord Justin of Kyle. At this point, Andrea had been brought hastily to London to participate in the ceremony, but her father and sister quarreled as to the wisdom of this step, and Pola had hinted at serious danger. From whom? And why? Andrea shook her head in exasperation. If only someone would confide in her! It seemed the only use her family had for her was as a source of money for their extravagances. Until now, Andrea had felt sorrow but no resentment at the cavalier treatment she usually received. But Pola's recent speeches and actions were becoming intolerable to a girl who was more now than a child, and who, in her school at least, had grown accustomed to a measure of affection and respect. She was, in point of fact, grateful for the impeccable social training the school had provided, as well as for the gentle concern and friendliness of several of her teachers. Her training was thorough enough to allow Andrea to realize the extent of her sister's self-willed flouting of convention and good taste—and worse, her utter insensitivity. Andrea, unlike those persons who came under the spell of Pola's vivid charm and high spirits, was not blinded to her sister's cruelty and selfishness.

The immediate cause of Andrea's resentment was her sister's behavior concerning the bridesmaid's costume. There was to be no rehearsal. Andrea's dress, ordered by Pola, had just arrived. The younger girl had been told to put it on and present herself for her sister's approval. The costume surprised Andrea. It was almost like a nun's habit—high neckline, long sleeves, full-gathered skirt just brushing the floor. In color it was palest green. With it came a pale green veil, floor length all around, which was held on Andrea's head by a circlet of white artificial flowers. Looking at herself in the small mirror above her bureau, Andrea felt anonymous. It could be anyone under that veil—or no one!

She ran downstairs and to the front of the house to her sister's suite. In her anger, she didn't knock, but threw open the door and entered in a swirl of pale green draperies. Pola, trying on a pair of diamond earrings which were part of a magnificent set the groom had sent her, glanced up with eyebrows raised in cool enquiry.

"I don't know why you bothered to send to Switzerland for me to attend you," the younger girl blurted out. "Any woman would have done as well, since this—this *costume* conceals my identity completely."

Pola's smile held malice. "You do look odd—like an animated candle-snuffer. But you'll have to direct your complaints to Vladi. He instructed the seamstress."

Andrea frowned. "Did *father* choose this dress for me?"

"As a matter of fact, little sister, he did. We agreed on the color and the general style." Pola pulled off the earrings, tossed them carelessly onto the dressing table, and clasped the heavy diamond necklace around her throat. "Since no one will be looking at anybody but me tomorrow, I fail to see what difference it makes how you look."

Sitting there in the light of a dozen candles in her satin and lace underclothing, Pola was an eye-filling, voluptuous creature. Her dark-red hair flowed down over her white shoulders, and her slanted green eyes glittered behind heavy white lids. An unfamiliar anger, ignited when Andrea had first seen the damping dowdiness of her green costume, now flared up hotly in her breast. Her outer manner became cooler, however, as she said slowly, "Am I to take it, then, that you both felt my person would embarrass you? Then why bring me here at all?"

"Oh, don't be tiresome, little sister. Your appearance means very little to anyone, since all eyes will be on me," she preened her lovely neck, making the diamonds around it sparkle with a hundred fires, "but of course, as the only other member of the family, you must be present." Andrea caught a wary look in the lustrous jade green eyes, but her sister was so unfamiliar to her that the younger girl could not read meaning into the glance.

The question she had been asking herself all this week came automatically to her lips. "Why did we come to London? Surely your friends and my father's are all in Warsaw?"

"That's true," said Pola with sudden anger. "And believe me, it won't be long before I'm back there, and in Paris, and all the places I hunger to visit! This time, with a wealthy husband to pay my bills." Pola laughed deep in her throat, a husky sound that Andrea knew she cultivated because she thought it was attractive to men. The older woman ran her eyes over the tall, slender figure standing before her. "You'd better learn that the smart huntsman goes where the game is. And Milord of Kyle is the biggest game there is!"

"You don't love him," Andrea stated.

"Of course not," Pola laughed. "But he's presentable and richer than Croesus. Richer even than you. Old, too—so he won't be too much trouble for me to handle."

"Old? How could father—?" Andrea protested.

Pola interrupted. "Oh, not *aged!* He's thirty-five." Since Pola, though she would not admit it, was twenty-six, Andrea was puzzled, and her expression revealed it. Pola looked sullen and snapped, "He's a cold, arrogant man. Doesn't look as though he'd ever smiled in his life. It's no wonder he hasn't been able to find a wife."

But Andrea had had to listen to Cousin Stacia's

interminable talk about the wealth, handsome face and figure, and superb lineage of the groom-to-be, and she scrutinized her sister's beautiful, self-indulgent face carefully. Why wasn't Pola in alt over the match? However she decried him, her affianced husband was admittedly the greatest catch of the season, a veritable nonpareil.

Was there someone else—a younger man, perhaps a Polish gentleman whose pretensions the count had depressed? Was this the reason for the trip to London and the quiet wedding? Andrea longed to ask her sister, but Pola's expression was closed and forbidding, and a moment later she sent the younger girl away.

The wedding itself was like a confused bad dream to Andrea. In the small ballroom, lighted by dozens of candles, her veil had as effectively prevented her seeing the few guests as them seeing her. Pola and Dominic Justin, a magnificently handsome couple, had paused only long enough to drink the conventional toasts and receive the congratulations of the guests before retiring to change clothing and set out at once for the groom's principal estate in Scotland. Andrea heard some murmurs of surprise and speculation about the hurried departure, usually followed, however, by a remark on the inflexible selfishness of Lord Justin, and less frequently by some ribald comment on his eagerness to get his wife to himself. Andrea had been startled, when it was all over and the guests had gone, to hear her father and Cousin Stacia congratulating each other on the successful speedy conclusion of the ceremony.

"Well, she ought to be safe enough now," vouchsafed Stacia.

Vladimir, catching sight of Andrea, said something quickly in a low voice and both of them turned to regard the girl. Wearily she removed the veil and dropped it onto a chair. The green dress and the long confinement under the veil did nothing to improve her appearance; she looked drained and lifeless. Vladimir frowned. She could see in his face that he was making a disparaging comparison between his two daughters.

"Green really isn't my best color," she offered, smiling a little pathetically.

"You looked very—suitable, child," said Stacia in an effort to be kind.

Vladimir shrugged and smothered a yawn.

"After so much excitement, I believe I'll seek a quiet evening at my club," he said, not quite looking at Andrea. "I'm sure you ladies will have a great deal to say to each other about the festivities. I bid you good evening." He strode off to his favorite club, The Foreigners, leaving Andrea feeling lonelier than she ever had in her life.

Chapter Three

ONE MORNING A MONTH LATER, Andrea waited until her father had left the house in his elegant curricle to go to The Foreigners Club, and Purvis the butler was in the cellar choosing the wine for dinner, before she sent the footman who was on duty at the front door to bring the carriage from the stables in the mews.

"Albert, you will please not inform anyone that I have gone out, especially Lady Stacia or Purvis. I am going to call upon Mrs. Drummond-Burrell, but I do not wish to make a great stir over the matter.

The young footman regarded her with admiration thoroughly mixed with concern. Nothing but a baby, Miss Andrea was, fresh out of her girl's school in foreign parts, and not up to any of the rigs and rows of Town, whatever she'd learned from her teachers. A far cry she was from that hot-at-hand piece her older sister, now safely married and vanished into the wilds of Scotland, to the devout relief of the household. But whatever Miss thought, Albert was well aware that the daughter of a count did not jaunter about the metropolis unattended, even to call upon one of the queens of London society,

23

the Patronesses of Almack's. Blot her copy right and proper, Miss Andrea would, if she didn't take care. With a sister like hers, the quizzies would jump on any peccadillo. Albert had heard of Mrs. Drummond-Burrell's icy respectability, and her refusal to forgive even the tiniest divergence from good *ton*. It was a nine-days wonder in the Town, her sponsorship of the Lady Pola. Count Vladi had a way with the ladies, no denying it! Proper charmer, the old boy! Mayhap the Burrell's kindness would extend to Miss Andrea. Reluctantly Albert did as he was ordered. He checked the girl's appearance as he handed her into the carriage. In spite of a very neat ankle, revealed as she stepped up into the vehicle, and a costume obviously of the first stare, Miss Andrea did not present a modish appearance. She was too slender and too tall. No feminine graces, Miss Andrea hadn't. Her clear amber gaze was too steady and open, more like a young lad's than a pretty girl's. Albert, himself a well-looking youth, thought critically that miss did not make enough of herself. What was the old lady up to, that she let miss rig herself out in clothes that didn't do a thing for her? Yet there was something very likeable in the small, stern face when it softened into a smile. That miss was going to such a reputable address as Mrs. Drummond-Burrell's town house reconciled Albert to seeing Andrea set out unaccompanied.

The girl sat back in the carriage and tried to marshal her thoughts. She knew that Mrs.

Burrell was the coldest and most strait-laced of the powerful Patronesses of Almack's—the Marriage Mart, as it was called in London—but the lady had introduced Pola into the beau monde when their father asked her to. Mrs. Drummond-Burrell had perhaps felt some softness for the handsome Polish aristocrat, for she had done a hitherto unprecedented thing and personally sponsored the motherless girl, launching her so successfully into the *haut ton* that Pola had snared that high-stickler, Lord Dominic Justin. For that reason Andrea had decided Mrs. Burrell might be the ideal person to advise Pola's sister in her dilemma.

Mrs. Burrell made no secret of her surprise at receiving a young woman unaccompanied by chaperone or abigail. Andrea, who was extremely nervous at the thought of the purpose behind her visit, found the lady's cold demeanor daunting. Plucking up her courage, however, she began in her pretty, low-voiced English,

"It is good of you to receive me, ma'am, on no notice whatever! But I have no mother, you see, and my chaperone, Mrs. Wasylyk, is—is not . . ."

"Your cousin Stacia is a widgeon," snapped Mrs. Burrell, "and is forever *talking*. It is no great wonder she never remarried."

"Just so, ma'am. However, I came because there is a matter which I cannot understand, and I hoped that you—"

"Let me have it in plain language, without bark on it, if you please," said the good dame impatiently.

Andrea took a deep breath. "In short, ma'am, can you tell me why my father brought us to London, and married off my sister so—so quietly?"

Mrs. Burrell pursed her lips with displeasure, but decided against giving one of her blighting snubs. How often had she regretted giving way to the cajoleries of that Polish charmer? Really, the whole affair was not in her style at all! Still, he was such a delightful man! She suppressed a sigh. Answer the chit, she told herself. She looks quite out of the average, as though she might be trusted to keep a secret . . . although why Vladimir hasn't told her—really, most annoying! This will teach you never to permit sensibility to overcome judgment, she thought.

"Your father wished your sister to be removed from the very fast set of young noblemen with whom he had surrounded himself in Warsaw. Knowing me, and my position in London society, he was convinced that I could sponsor your sister and arrange a suitable match. Which I must say I did." She had surprised even herself when she brought Kyle up to scratch. A triumph, considering Lord Justin's well-known disinterest in the sex. "Kyle's mother was just such a one as your sister, very hot-at-hand, which may be the reason for Lord Justin's reluctance to wed. But Pola, besides being criminally lovely, is awake on all suits, and caught his fancy. He could never have endured an insipid miss for five minutes. Men, my dear," confided Mrs.

Burrell in an unaccustomed access of plain-speaking, "are easily bored by good women! Of course Vladimir was delighted to have her safely married to Kyle. No one would dare to breathe a word against Lord Dominic Justin's wife!"

Andrea, not quite sure this last was a compliment to Pola, was nevertheless relieved at an explanation which she could accept as possible. "Thank you. I wondered a little at the whole affair," she confessed.

"And are you now at ease in your mind?"

Andrea let her clear gaze rest on the hooded eyes of the older woman. "I am most grateful for your courtesy and forbearance to one who had no right to intrude upon your privacy," the girl said quietly. "I know I am very green, but I think I am not stupid. It has seemed to me of late that my father was troubled. This might be because we have heard nothing from Pola since she left on her wedding day, although all of us have written to her every week. There was a note from Lord Justin, my father says, but only to inform us of their safe arrival at Kyle Castle."

"Is your sister a devoted correspondent? I would not have thought it," said Mrs. Burrell.

"No," admitted Andrea. "I have never received a letter from her in my life."

"Your father shows concern?" persisted Mrs. Burrell.

Andrea's pale gold eyebrows drew slightly together. "Papa does not admit to being concerned. In fact, he speaks quite sharply to Cousin Stacia when she has been going on about it—"

"Vladimir has all my sympathy! That cousin of yours—!" Mrs. Burrell shuddered. "Yet still you feel he is worried at not hearing from your sister?"

"He does not share his thoughts with me, and indeed I know I have not the right to demand enlightenment. Good children should be seen but not heard," she concluded with a small smile.

Mrs. Burrell was not a woman easily moved to compassion. She had to admit, however, that this child, so grave of demeanor, so classically exquisite of feature, had in some sort moved her. She looked more searchingly at the small, fine-boned face. Really remarkable eyes, she decided. She is better looking than I had at first thought. Perhaps in a few years . . .

"How old are you, child? And what is your name?"

"I am Andrea, and I am seventeen."

Good again! No missish airs. Almost too direct a manner, perhaps, for best style, but a welcome relief from coy and giggling maidens. "I like you, Andrea," Mrs. Burrell was surprised to hear herself admit. "Have Vladimir bring you to me in a year and I shall see what I can do for you."

Andrea excused herself with the proper expressions of gratitude, and took her departure in correct form. "The chit's been well-taught," was Mrs. Burrell's final judgment before she put the whole matter out of her cold, well-disciplined mind.

Arriving home half an hour later, Andrea walked into tragedy. Her first inkling was the sight of her father's curricle standing before the door unattended, with a small crowd of strangers clustered on the pavement beside it. She rang, but Purvis was not there to swing open the door for her. The door stayed stubbornly closed. A red-faced Albert let her in after she had rung the bell several times. He had his mouth open to berate the bell-ringer before he realized who she was. Then his face became the smooth mask of the well-trained servant, and he said only, "I didn't tell him where you'd gone, miss. You'd better go up to your father's room."

With this cryptic utterance he closed the front door and went to the small spy-hole which her father had had installed in order that the servants could observe who stood upon the doorstep before opening the door. Albert had obviously not been at his post when first Andrea rang the bell. This departure from established custom was more disturbing than his words. However, the girl did not pause to decipher the meaning of his first remark. She ran up the great stairway at a pace Mrs. Burrell would have roundly condemned. She hurried down the central hallway toward her father's suite.

Within his bedroom there were several servants, including Purvis, and two strange gentlemen. One of these, who was bending over a body on the bed, seemed to be a doctor. Andrea caught her breath. The body on the bed was Count Vladimir's.

"What is going on? Has my father been hurt?"

Everyone in the room turned to speak to her at once. She held up her hand, addressing the man who bent over her father. "You are a doctor, sir?"

"Belwin, Edward Belwin, at your service milady. Your father has had an accident."

"Accident!" exclaimed the other stranger with lively indignation. "That's wrapping it up in fine linen! This gentleman was murdered!"

The doctor cast a warning glance, and Purvis an affronted one, at the accuser. Andrea stared at him with horror. He was a young man, dressed in sober good style rather than à la modality. His rather plain face was tense with emotion. Disregarding the warning frowns of the doctor and the butler, he addressed himself to Andrea.

"I was there, ma'am. Present when the 'accident' occurred. There was a grubby rascal holding the horses outside your father's club. I was walking down St. James's Street, approaching the vehicle, and of course I noticed the horses. Thought it rash to trust such a nervous, high-bred pair to the care of a hulking lout. Then your father came out of his club, walked down the steps, flung the grubby fellow a coin and said, 'Stand to their heads till I give you the office,' and prepared to mount up into the curricle." The speaker took a much crumpled handkerchief from his pocket and wiped his forehead. "Happened like a flash! Fellow jabbed something into the near horse just as your father went off balance, mounting. He fell to the pavement heavily, and the—the murderer backed the horses over him!"

"That will be quite enough, sir!" ordered the doctor, angrily. The girl, white-faced, was swaying a little. Purvis was at her side in an instant.

"Let me lead you to your room, Miss Andrea. I'll send your abigail to you. Lady Stacia is driving out, but I'll have her attend you the instant she returns."

Andrea swallowed hard. "Thank you, Purvis, but I must see my father first."

Purvis' glance queried the doctor. The latter shrugged.

"If there is no older immediate relative in the house? Very well, then." He stood aside reluctantly from the head of the bed. Andrea came forward and looked steadily down upon her father.

The doctor had drawn a sheet up so that only Count Vladimir's face was revealed. There was a deep gash at one side of his head, partly concealed by the damp, still-dark hair. The count's face was very peaceful, very pale, the eyes closed. Andrea took one look and then her glance flew to the doctor's face.

"He is—dead?" she whispered.

"Yes, I regret to say. He was dead when I

arrived. No one could have saved him. The massive internal injuries alone ... and there was that blow to the head—"

Andrea swayed against Purvis' arm.

"You have to thank this young man," the doctor continued. "He obtained your father's address from the club doorman, enlisted the services of a servant to help him, and brought your father here."

Purvis had had enough. "I'll just take Miss Andrea to her room," he said, grimly eyeing the medico. "Perhaps you might wish to leave a sedative draught?"

"Of course," muttered the doctor. "I'll follow you. There's nothing more I can do here."

It was not until late that evening that Andrea learned the full extent of her loss. A letter which had been sitting upon the elegant carved table beside a bowl of roses in the hall, forgotten in the stirring crisis and confusion, was found by Purvis and given to Lady Stacia with her dinner. She read it and lost color. Signalling to the butler, she held it out for him to read. This most unconventional behavior was excusable, perhaps, for the poor lady, never too bright at the best of times, had now no one closer than the drugged girl upstairs with whom to share her burdens. Purvis, rising to the emergency, had functioned as steward as well as butler, managing all the details during that dreadful day with resource and poise. As he absorbed the contents of the missive, however, even the imperturbable Purvis blanched.

"Not Miss Pola, too!—Lady Justin, I should say," he corrected himself.

"What is happening to us?" whispered Lady Stacia.

Immediately Purvis regained his composure. "You'll have to tell Miss Andrea, of course, but I should advise waiting until tomorrow morning."

"Yes, yes!" agreed Lady Stacia. "The potion worked well. She is sleeping so peacefully . . . I couldn't bear to awaken her just to tell her that her sister is dead too. Oh, this day!" The poor lady broke into a string of Polish phrases and rocked herself slightly back and forth in her chair.

This will never do, thought Purvis. Next thing, we'll have one of the footmen in here and the whole household will fall apart. He went to the sideboard and poured a stiff shot of brandy. Taking it to Lady Stacia, he cleared his throat with enough force to obtain the poor creature's attention.

"You must be strong, madam," he said firmly. "Not only Miss Andrea but all the staff depend now upon your vision and strength."

The distraught lady looked up at her servant through tear-washed eyes. She caught her breath on a sob, and then stammered, "On me? Yes, that's true. The child has no one else now. Oh, Purvis, what am I to do?"

Good, thought Purvis. I can handle it if she doesn't fall into the vapors. Proffering the brandy, he said, "You must drink this to recruit your strength, and then you must write a note to the count's man of law. I shall see it is delivered first thing in the morning. And then, may I suggest that you retire? Miss Andrea will need all your help to support her through tomorrow."

Lady Stacia drained the whole of the large glass of brandy Purvis had poured for her, and began to feel a little better. "Yes, I'll take your advice, Purvis. Write the note to Parsnell; go to bed and try to sleep. Must be ready to comfort Andrea."

"But not tonight," said Purvis quietly. "In the morning, when you're both rested."

"Yes. Good thinking. In the morning."

Purvis himself escorted the lady to her bedroom, where he gave her into the care of her dresser. There was no need for comment between these excellently-trained servants.

Chapter Four

ANDREA SAT ALONE in the room which had been her father's study. Two weeks had passed since the day she had returned home from Mrs. Burrell's mansion to find him dead. The news of Pola's death by misadventure had been less of a shock, since her senses were already numbed by the first loss. On the desk in front of the girl was the letter from Lord Dominic Justin. It was addressed to her father, and seemed to Andrea to be the coldest, most heartless missive she had ever read.

My dear Count Wasylyk: I deeply regret having to inform you that your daughter has been killed in an accident. She was riding a new horse, and apparently lost control of the animal. There was a storm raging, and it was some time before the stableman informed me she had the horse out. She was dead at the foot of Castle Cliff when I found her.

You have, sir, my deepest sympathy in your loss. My steward, Alan, who bears this, will wait upon you tomorrow to learn whether it is your wish to come to Kyle Castle to see your daughter's grave. The interment cannot be delayed until your arrival, since the state of the English roads is such that a journey of several days is required to reach Kyle by coach.

Again, my condolences and regrets.

It was signed with a slashing JUSTIN.

No word of Pola—of his love and personal sorrow! Trying to control her anger at the man's insensitivity, Andrea began to consider a course of action. She had denied herself to all callers during the past two weeks, permitting Cousin Stacia to receive them in her stead. But she was beginning to feel irked by her seclusion. She faced the fact that her grief was becoming overshadowed by a rising suspicion. Who was the "hulking lout" who had, perhaps accidentally, perhaps deliberately, caused her father's death? He had never been seen again, nor had a careful search by the Bow Street Runners turned up any clue to his identity.

And then there was the even more unlikely accident to Pola, a superb horsewoman, accustomed to riding mountain trails in any kind of weather. Was it only a gruesome coincidence that she had died in exactly the same manner as her mother?

Andrea pulled herself up sharply. What was she thinking? That someone had planned a murder—*two murders?* To her surprise, she found that she was convinced, for whatever vague, irrational reasons, that Pola's death had been no accident, but murder. She thought back carefully over the whole series of events since she had been so hastily summoned to England to play a role in the wedding of her sister. Why London? Why the small guest list? Why the hasty departure of the newly-married couple? Why no answers to the letters she and her father had sent to Pola? And finally, why the repetitious character of the tragedy?

Her father's reticence about family affairs she was forced to discount. He had never really shared anything with her except his name, and occasionally his home. So the fact that she had felt him to be under some kind of strain in the few weeks they had been together in London was not a significant element in the puzzle which confronted her . . . the *deadly* puzzle, if her suspicions were correct.

Andrea frowned. Whom could she consult for answers to her questions? It was unthinkable that she should approach Mrs. Drummond-Burrell again, although that lady had meticulously observed all the correct forms in sending flowers and letters of condolence. Who, then?

Cousin Stacia, of course! The older woman had revealed unexpected strength in the two weeks just past, rising to the emergency with a command she had never before displayed. Andrea got up, and folding Lord Justin's letter, placed it in her reticule. Then she went out into the hall to discover the whereabouts of her cousin.

Stacia was found in the ladies' parlor, where she sat embroidering a cushion and enjoying the sunlight from an open French window. Her face lighted up with pleasure as Andrea entered.

"So boring, embroidery, I always think," she began, smiling. "I've done it for so many years it has become almost second nature, yet I must confess I never really enjoyed it. Nor," regarding her rather straggly design, "have I ever learned to do it well. But you didn't come in to listen to me chattering about my wretched needlework! What's troubling you, child?"

"I need to talk to you about the family." Now that she had actually initiated the topic, it seemed difficult for Andrea to admit her suspicions.

Cousin Stacia was regarding her closely. "Of course, child. What did you wish to know?"

Andrea took the plunge boldly. "I find that I am unable to accept as coincidence the fact that my father and my sister died of supposed accidents within the same week."

Instead of uttering cries of distress, or presenting a facade of ignorance, Cousin Stacia considered Andrea's challenge coolly. At length she replied, "I must confess some such suspicion had entered my own mind. Would you like to tell me your ideas about this tragedy?"

Andrea, grateful for the unexpected support, carefully related her own doubts. When she had faltered to a close, her cousin nodded slowly.

"I agree. There is much which must be explained, or at the least, more clearly examined. To add to what you say, I have some other details. Albert told me a tall man had come to enquire for you and your father just after you had left this house. Mindful of his promise to you, Albert declined to divulge where you had gone, but saw no reason not to inform this plausible, well-dressed stranger of your father's whereabouts. From this I deduce that the stranger was a man of some address, since Albert is such a snob that he would never give any information to one he considered to be outside your father's social circle."

Andrea was amazed. "However did you find all this out, Cousin Stacia? If Albert refused to confide in the stranger—I had gone to call on Mrs. Drummond-Burrell, by the way—how did you get him to tell you anything?"

"I have my ways of obtaining information," the older woman said with a certain complacency. "My point is that this enquiring stranger has never returned. Of this I am quite sure."

"Could it have been Milord Justin's steward?" suggested Andrea.

Stacia shook her head. "That good man, by name Alan, waited upon me the day after your father's death. He behaved just as he ought, and said all that was fitting in the situation. La, Andrea!" Stacia gurgled, her eyes sparkling, "he was a fine figure of a man, big and solid and with that terribly *male* dignity!" She sighed. "Just about my age, too. I grow exceedingly tired of being ages older than all the men I meet!"

Andrea found herself in considerable sympathy with her cousin. "In my case, *they* are all too old," she observed, "or I am too young."

"At least yours is a handicap which will diminish with time," retorted Stacia. "Now where were we? Oh, yes, the mysterious stranger! Albert saw Alan when he came, and avers that he was not the enquiring stranger." She paused, frowning. "Oh, I begin to see where your suspicions are leading you." Her eyes opened very wide. "Can it be that you think Lord Justin might have been instrumental in causing the death of his wife and his father-in-law? I cannot think it! For what should be his reasons?"

Andrea was relieved to note that her cousin had shown none of the conventional horrified rejection of the idea which might have been expected. Truly, the older woman was revealing unsuspected strengths!

"I hadn't got that far in my speculations," the girl admitted. "Could it be the dowry?"

"Oh, no! Lord Justin was the giver, not the receiver. The settlement which he made upon your sister was princely. And from all I hear, he need hardly regard even that sum. He is tremendously wealthy."

"Then why would he wish to kill my sister and my father? Can you not think of the reason, Stacia?" persisted the girl.

Her cousin regarded her with a troubled gaze. "You seem so sure that it was *he* who did so. Yet I cannot think of a single reason why he should wish to. Far more likely that it was just a tragic coincidence, or even that some trouble from Vladi's past, or Pola's, should have found its resolution here."

"That is what I hoped you might be able to tell me," Andrea said. "I know so little of my family ... you know I have scarcely spent a month in any year together with them since I was nine years old. I have no knowledge of their affairs, their hopes, their fears!"

Stacia pursed her lips. "It is your right to know as much as I can tell you," she decided, "although I must admit that neither of them ever confided in me. Your sister has always been a wilful, difficult girl. Just, I may add, like her mother. Vladi never would make the slightest effort to control her. Indeed, I often thought he urged her on, enjoyed her outrageous exploits." Stacia brooded darkly. "The Wasylyks have ever been wild creatures, proud of their excesses. You, on the other hand, much resemble your excellent mama, a delightful woman who could have done wonders with your father, had she lived. But you are right. I too, have often wondered why we came so unexpectedly to London. I must tell you that Pola's name was being bandied about in Warsaw society, and whatever Vladi's shortcomings, lack of family pride was not one of them."

"My sister was notorious?" whispered Andrea.

"Oh, most people forgave her her unconventional behavior; the men because of her beauty, the women because of her lineage. Also because all the female social arbiters were nutty upon

Vladi, and he played up to them," Stacia added knowledgeably. "The best thing about Vladi was that he really liked women, and entered into their concerns with interest."

"Except mine," Andrea found herself saying. "He's hardly spoken to me fifty times in my life."

"Yes, well—" Cousin Stacia was disconcerted. Then she said vaguely, "Of course a daughter is bound to be different, especially such a young one. I have not a doubt in the world that he would have come to a very good understanding with you, as he did with Pola, now that you are growing older."

"Then I have Milord Justin to thank for cheating me of that pleasure," said Andrea bitterly.

Stacia considered her soberly. "You really feel that Lord Dominic Justin is a murderer, child? How should you have formed such an adverse opinion on the basis of a few hours' acquaintance?"

"That is, in some cases, I am persuaded, enough and more than enough time. The man is cold, arrogant, indifferent to the feelings of others," Andrea averred hotly. "And as if his manner were not sufficient, there is this letter. I challenge you to tell me this is the letter of a bereaved bridegroom!"

Stacia shook her head. "You place too much weight upon a formal condolence, child. Many men seek to hide their emotions under a facade of strength and indifference. I believe the

English call it keeping a stiff upper lip. English noblemen—and Scotsmen, too, I imagine, as they go to the same schools—consider it demeaning to betray deep emotion in public."

"A letter of condolence to one's father-in-law can hardly be called a public disclosure!" protested Andrea.

"True; yet think, child, if he had indeed killed his wife of a month, why would he hasten to London by stealth and murder the very father to whom he was writing this note of condolence which has you so in a pucker?"

Andrea shrugged. "Who can say, with such a man? But I have decided one thing, Cousin Stacia. I am going to Kyle Castle and seek for myself the full story of Pola's death."

"Impossible!" breathed her cousin, horror-stricken. "You are not out of mourning, and will not be for a year—by which time all clues will be cold or removed," she added, practically. "You are a young girl, alone, not yet out in society. What possible excuse could you give for such a journey? No," she went on hastily, "do not tell me you will propose to go to comfort your sister's husband in his grief, for I've a strong notion he isn't the kind of man who'd appreciate that kind of attention!"

"I had not intended to go as myself, or to advertise the connection," said Andrea, as calmly as if the idea had not just presented itself to her.

Stacia was betrayed into an open-mouthed stare.

Warming to her theme, Andrea elaborated. "I'll wear man's clothing, cut off my hair, send a small trunk ahead to Kyle and ride the new mare father just bought me—"

"Not a mare, child," objected Stacia. "The men of your family would ride only stallions. Besides, what possible reason could you give for turning up at Kyle Castle?"

"Oh, I won't present myself at the Castle," said Andrea, improvising airily. "I'll stay at a local inn, something quiet and unpretentious, and say I am writing a book or something. That should excuse my questioning the locals—"

"Nonsense," said Stacia, dampening enthusiasm. "Writing a book, indeed! A wretched excuse! You'd better be studying something—the local legends, or history of the Justin family—no, that would rouse too much interest and cause you to be subjected to particular attention. I think your best plan would be to give it out that you are studying something innocuous and quite impersonal, like flora and fauna of southern Scotland, or clams, or something equally dull."

Andrea gazed at her cousin with delight. "Why have you never been like this before, Stacia? Or have you, and I just was not home enough to really appreciate you?"

Stacia blushed becomingly. "I truly believe I have achieved a new lease on life. Perhaps it is being forced to manage the household, to make the decisions, to be finally *important* in someone's life . . . Dear child, I'd like to go with you on your quest, foolhardy though it appears to

44

me to be. Dangerous, too. You must remember," her voice became grave, "your sister Pola was extravagant and fiery-tempered, but it was not those qualities which made her the talk of the Warsaw. She was, though I regret to tell you of it, a wicked girl. She delighted in arousing her numerous suitors to excesses of emotion and then laughing at them. She pitted one youth against another—the duels she caused!—then quite ruthlessly discarded both when a more interesting prospect appeared. It was in the cards that such an end as she has suffered should befall her. Possibly she tried her new husband's patience too far—he looked an arrogant, unforgiving creature, it is true! But we did not think disaster would reach her here, in England, where she was scarcely known. Yet how quickly one's past catches up to one! I myself overheard a quizzy female discussing Pola at Almack's one evening. 'She is a great deal too wild and coming, in spite of her noble birth,' the lady was confiding to her friends, 'Milady Hot-at-Hand, I hear they call her in the gentlemen's clubs! Someone ought to warn Justin what he's getting into!' And then all the quizzies smirked and grimaced knowingly, and one of them said, 'It won't hurt that starched-up creature to be taken down a peg or two! Our own lovely English girls aren't good enough for him. Let's see how he handles this outrageous lady!' I trembled for Pola, and for your father, but apparently no one had the brass to gossip to Milord Justin about his fiancée."

"Perhaps someone did, too late, and he took his revenge," suggested Andrea, narrow-eyed.

"No, I am sure you are mistaken, child. Such ideas come from reading too many lending library romances. In real life, things never happen so interestingly," chided her cousin.

To which Andrea replied, "But father is dead, and so is Pola! And I must find out what truly occurred, for I cannot accept that both would die by ill-chance within a few days of one another."

"You may be right, child," admitted Stacia. "And if so, the murderer must be brought to justice. But do you not think perhaps the Bow Street Runners—?" She answered her own question before Andrea could speak. "No, of course not. The matter must have no public airing. Too much that is harmful to our family could be disclosed. You must try to find out what you can, but I beg of you, Andrea, take no risks. Be content to discover the truth if you can. Then come to me with what you have learned, and we shall decide what is to be done about it."

It did not occur to either of these nobly-born ladies that the course upon which the younger one was embarking was not only supremely dangerous if their suspicions were correct, but also quite unacceptable as the conduct of a well-bred girl. Cousin Stacia, as well as being bird-witted, was rather flown with her own emerging importance and competence in a household where she had so long been little regarded. And Andrea had had no experience whatever of the great world she now proposed to enter in a disguise which laid her open to embarrassments she was too naive to envision. She did not entertain for a moment the notion that she herself might become a byword in polite society, or be considered a lady even more hot-at-hand than her notorious sister.

Chapter Five

TO HER CREDIT, Stacia did suffer a few qualms as she abetted Andrea in her design to investigate Pola's death. Unfortunately, her scruples were not sufficiently powerful to cause her to put an end to the ill-advised scheme. Her life had been so circumscribed by her humble position in the family that she was quite carried away by this opportunity to act boldly, and all the suppressed fervors of her widowed existence were suddenly rampant.

There was much to be thought of. All must be done without the servants' knowledge, which fact presented, as both ladies were well aware, almost insuperable obstacles. Challenged, and, if it be admitted, more than a little pleased at the clandestine nature of their activities, the older lady revealed Machiavellian duplicity in the execution of their unconventional plan. First she caused it to be set abroad in the household that Miss Andrea was returning to her school in Switzerland for a time, to restore her shattered nerves in familiar and cloistered surroundings. To prepare for the trip, it was essential to shop for a more suitable wardrobe for the girl. Thus with complete propriety Andrea and her cousin were driven to various establishments purveying clothing. If Tom Coachman wondered at the less than exclusive character of the shops of their choice, naturally he said nothing beyond a casual remark in servants' hall to the effect that the old dame was a bit of a pinch-penny. Milord would have had his daughter to the finest modiste in London, he opined. To which Purvis retorted that since Miss was supposed to be in mourning, and a schoolgirl at that, it was quite suitable she be dressed sober-like.

Thus turned loose in the Pantheon Bazaar and similar places, the ladies purchased clothing for a mythical twin brother who happened to be exactly the size of Andrea. Later, while the servants were safely occupied at their dinner, Andrea packed their purchases in a modest portmanteau and the small trunk which had held her schoolgirl wardrobe.

"I sha'n't be a top-of-the-trees dandy, nor even point-device," she sighed as she folded the sober blue cloth coat and breeches.

Cousin Stacia was betrayed into a titter quite unsuitable for a proper duenna. "My love, have you *considered?* Your appearance in these garments, I mean! Should anyone recognize you in such attire, you would be quite disgraced."

Andrea regarded the breeches with approval. "I really can find it in my heart to envy males, when I consider the freedom and comfort of their attire. Only think, Cousin Stacia! No layers of clinging skirts to hamper and hobble one, no tight-laced stays, no garlands of shawls and lappets and rattling necklaces to bind and distract! It is a matter of wonder to me that women have not rebelled against the confinement of their attire!"

"Never dare to breathe such heresy, child!" advised her chaperone. Then she smiled. "It's a blessing you're practically unknown in London, and an even greater one that you will be carrying out this masquerade in the far north, whence, I daresay, few even of the gentry ever get up to Town. There's no chance you'll be recognized," she comforted herself.

"Even had every soul in Kyle Village been a regular visitor to London, I should be in no danger, for I was kept so close that no one but our own servants ever really saw me," As she spoke, Andrea was stuffing more garments into her trunk. "I'll take both pairs of my riding breeches and boots. Thank Heaven my father didn't decide to put me in a lady's habit till I reached London."

One of Count Vladimir's special concerns had been that both his daughters be taught to ride Cossack style, astride. Although this shocked both his own social circle and Andrea's school-teachers, he had insisted. He was resolved to have no more such dreadful accidents as the one which cost him his beloved first wife. The death of Pola's mother had caused him to prefer the safety of a proper seat upon the animal over the mincing propriety of side-saddles and draped skirts. So both daughters were taught to ride by a former cavalry officer, and both had habits made in the masculine style by the count's own tailor.

The night before the two ladies were to set out for Dover—for Cousin Stacia had spread it abroad that she was conducting Andrea to meet a teacher there—the cutting of Andrea's long golden hair was accomplished, not without sentimental tears on the older woman's part. "This is sacrilege," she murmured as her scissors sheared through the heavy, shining layers.

Andrea was too young, or too lacking in vanity, to mourn. "No scholar of the male persuasion would be found with a head of flowing hair," Andrea told her. "I should be forever worrying lest my hat should fall off and the whole mass come tumbling down about my shoulders."

Stacia shuddered at the thought of that contretemps, then chuckled irrepressibly. "What a start it would give everyone within viewing distance," she said.

"Especially if it occurred in a tavern," added Andrea.

"A *tavern!*" almost shrieked her cousin. "You cannot mean it, my love! I must refuse to let you take one step outside the door until you swear to me that you will never put foot in such a place!"

"I think you are right. The young student I shall be impersonating would have neither the funds nor the time to waste in roistering." Unaware of her cousin's incredulous stare, she peered at her shorn head in the mirror. "I think you have done an excellent job of it." The short hair was beginning to reveal a tendency to curl. She brushed it into her conception of a fashionable style. "Now, the hat!" she announced, lifting a curly-brimmed beaver from its box, she set it at a careful angle on the short curls. Regarding her image with complacency, she said, "I look the complete gentleman."

Stacia pursed her lips. "Very handsome, young sir. You'll have half the maidens in sight swooning after you."

"God forbid," intoned Andrea piously, then broke into a chuckle. "I have also thought that I must practice speaking in a lowered voice, and not squeaking if I should see a mouse."

"Lud, child, do you do so? Squeak, I mean. I would not have thought it of you!"

They joined in a laugh, but Stacia was secretly much struck with Andrea's appearance. In truth, she made a prettier man than she had a girl. Was it the soft head of golden curls, which revealed the beautiful line of chin and throat as the heavy mass of long, hanging hair had never done? Or was it the new air of excitement which brought a flush of color to the pale cheeks and a light of interest and determination to the great amber eyes, black-lashed, which had been the one notable feature of the stern, fine-boned face? Whatever it was, Andrea made a handsome youth, and Stacia began to wonder, too late, about the propriety of what they were attempting. For no one, man or woman, with eyes in his head, would fail to notice the re-markably good-looking boy; or, having noticed, fail to question.

Andrea was already sweeping up the long golden locks from the floor and consigning them to the fire. There was a good draught, so the smoke was drawn up the chimney, and only the faintest reek of burnt hair lingered in the room. The small portmanteau was packed with the white shirts and handkerchiefs they had pur-chased, the lengths of soft cloth Andrea had bought to bind up her young breasts, and the underwear which Stacia had blushed over.

"We forgot an overcoat, my child! You'll need something warm and durable if you plan to ride north," advised Stacia.

"I'll wear one of my father's. He has a hunt-ing coat that he wore in the rain. It is short and has two small shoulder capes. I remember it from last winter, at the castle."

"But will he have packed it? Is it here?" worried Stacia.

"We must go and see while the servants are still at table," decided Andrea. The two ladies crept down the hall to the heavily-shrouded apartments formerly occupied by the count. Here, after prudently locking the door, they rummaged in the massive wardrobes and found a short driving coat which pleased Andrea better than the garment of her first choice. Although she had doffed the beaver in her own room, hiding it in its box, and was wearing one of her new black gowns, the driving coat looked very well, if a trifle large. It gave her slight frame a bulkiness it did not actually possess, and was so modish that it turned the girl into quite a smart figure of young manhood, as Cousin Stacia was pleased to comment.

"Bravo!" she smiled. "I vow I could fall quite in love with you, child, in that garment! How lucky men are to be able to wear really warm coats of such style. I swear I half freeze in my silks and laces when I go abroad in this wretched climate!"

"I do look well," decided Andrea, posturing in front of her father's large cheval glass. She rummaged a little further, and found some fine cravats and a pair of beautiful soft leather riding gloves. They were not much too large, the Court having possessed a slender, elegant hand, so she appropriated them. His boots were too big, and she eyed the shining rows of them with frustration. "As things stand, I have only my two pairs of riding boots and those ridiculous slippers you purchased for me at the Pantheon," she whispered as they tiptoed back to Andrea's room.

"I couldn't resist the tigers embroidered on the toes, my love," confessed Stacia. "No one will ever see them, for you'll wear them only in your bedroom."

"They will be comfortable after a day spent in riding boots," the girl agreed. "Thank you, dear Stacia, for everything!"

"I only hope we don't both live to regret this wild venture," said her cousin, gloomily. The sight of the girl in a man's greatcoat had shaken her more than she cared to admit. Andrea was so small, and the coat was so big. The coat, and the world, she thought anxiously. What was she letting the child run into? But she knew enough of this young, little regarded cousin to understand her will and high courage, and to respect the quiet poise learned through years of loneliness and rejection.

The transfer went with ease. The two ladies, shepherded by Tom Coachman and two footmen, were safely ensconced in the largest, busiest inn at Dover. They had adjoining rooms, and kept the inn maids running up and down with hot water and tea trays and ridiculous errands until everyone was heartily sick of these demanding guests and kept out of their way as much as possible. Having encouraged that attitude deliberately, the ladies then proceeded to put their scheme into action.

Andrea changed into masculine clothing in her room, checked her well-filled purse, and walked quietly downstairs and out a side door at an hour when the mail-coach was just discharging its passengers. In the bustle, no one took note of a slim youth who might have been visiting someone at the inn. Once free of the hostel, the youth proceeded to a public stable where the ladies had noticed horses were being offered for sale, since it appeared that gentlemen occasionally rode to the port and disposed of their mount before boarding the boat for France.

Andrea chose a small, neatish black with a wise and gentle eye, who answered to the name of Boyo. She purchased a saddle and gear and rode off to the modest inn they had chosen for the transfer. The small trunk and portmanteau were already there, delivered by a bored ostler who thought more of the tip he got than the job he was doing. So "Mr. Tad Bartholomew" took up a brief and unexceptional residence in the house, and keep very much to himself until he had arranged to have his few possessions delivered to Kyle Village within the week. Then he set forward upon his journey, riding Boyo and accompanied by the prayers and guilty apprehension of Cousin Stacia.

Chapter Six

YOUNG MR. TAD BARTHOLOMEW found himself very comfortably accommodated at The Stag, the smaller and less pretentious of Kyle Village's two charming inns. As she had explained to Cousin Stacia, Andrea could be sure that the name of Tadeuz Bartolomeu, her maternal grandfather—the mine-owner—was one name Count Vladi would not have mentioned to his high-in-the-instep son-in-law. The Stag offered excellent meals served in a low-ceilinged dining room whose small-paned windows overlooked a charming garden. The landlord, whose name was Applegate, was pleased to have a guest who planned to stay for several weeks. Mistress Applegate thought the young scholar a very pretty gentleman, quiet and well-behaved, not like some of the young swells who frequently made the night hideous with their racket at the Kyle Arms, the larger hostelry.

Mr. Bartholomew was pleased to approve his neat bedroom with its two dormer windows, flowered curtains against whitewashed walls, and a narrow, comfortable bed. After the servant had deposited the new guest's small trunk and given thanks for the gratuity, Andrea locked her door and placed the contents of her port-manteau and most of the things from her trunk in the commodious dresser. She left the long green bridesmaid's dress and veil in the trunk under secure lock.

She had packed these two items in her trunk while Stacia was otherwise occupied. She had not wished her cousin to know of the dangerous plan which had occurred to her. If all other means of securing information failed, Andrea had decided to cause Pola's ghost to ride at night, and observe the reaction of the villagers and the residents of the castle. That would make them talk! The appearance of his murdered wife should give Milord Arrogance something to think about! Meanwhile, she locked the trunk, and added the key to the two rings she wore on a chain around her neck. They were her father's signet and her mother's wedding ring. In a small box in her drawer, along with a few rather trumpery fobs which might plausibly belong to a young student, she kept the magnif-icent topaz and diamond pendant which had been her father's gift to his second wife on the occasion of their marriage. Count Vladi had presented it to Andrea on her sixteenth birth-day, remarking that the topaz matched her eyes. She valued it above any other possession.

Having thus bestowed her gear, Andrea in the person of Mr. Tad Bartholomew sallied out to stroll through the village. It was set in the midst of wide fields and meadows, a smiling valley rising through a forest to the cliff which protected it on the west side from the battering of ocean winds. On top of that western cliff, and dominating the valley, was Kyle Castle, massive and gray and built with a medieval splendor of towers and battlements.

Turning her back resolutely on this evidence of Lord Justin's power, Andrea walked along the highroad toward the center of the village. She was forced to admit that Milord Justin was master of a pleasant demesne. Neat cottages behind low stone walls boasted thrifty kitchen gardens. There was a well-planned smithy with a burly, smiling blacksmith in a kilt. There was a small kirk with the graveyard behind it, and the manse nearby. The small shops were well-kept and displayed merchandise of good quality. At the center of the village, the larger inn, calling itself the Kyle Arms and displaying a board painted with a black sword on a scarlet shield, was of impressive size and excellent maintenance. Just north of the village, from an outcrop of the same rock on which Kyle Castle was built, a sturdy stream fell down the cliff, turning the wheel for an efficient-looking mill below.

Young Mr. Bartholomew made a couple of minor purchases, and tried to sound out the proprietors about their overlord. Though they gave courteous and respectful attention to the young customer, that was all they gave him; for every encroaching question there was an evasive answer. Andrea began to realize that this would take longer than she had anticipated. She left the small cluster of shops feeling irritated at the smiling men and women with their charming soft Scots' accent and their annoying habit of chatting pleasantly while saying nothing of use to her. With a sigh, she went back to The Stag for another delicious meal. "I shall be a fat old woman before I discover what I came to learn," she thought crossly.

In the next few days, Andrea was careful to go out every morning into the meadows and woods and along the hedgerows for a couple of hours, carrying her notebook and drawing pencils, and collecting specimens of wild flowers, leaves and even weeds. Botany had been a favorite study of hers in Switzerland, and one of her teachers had encouraged her to begin a collection and study the subject. She was grateful for her old notebook with its carefully inked drawings and notes.

Returning to the inn from one of such trips a few days after her arrival, she found a strange man was to share the meal with her.

"Mr. Bartholomew, this is Mr. William," said Applegate. "Like yourself, young sir, he finds The Stag a good place for his work. I'll wager you're sharp-set after a morning in the open air! I'll tell Cook you're ready for your meal," and he bustled off to the kitchen.

"What is your work, Mr. Bartholomew?" the man enquired, as soon as Applegate had left the room.

"I am a student on vacation from college," Andrea told him. "I am collecting materials for a paper on the wild flowers of this region of Scotland."

The girl felt some apprehension that she might be expected to spend some time in the company of this man. She scrutinized him covertly. He seemed to be about thirty, a dark, handsome fellow of medium height. His hands were well-kept but hard and muscular. He had an attractive white smile. Andrea guessed he was a favorite with the ladies. As he sat down at the table, Andrea caught a faint whiff of spicy fragrance. A dandy, she thought, and assuredly a squire of dames. She decided to study him.

Remembering to use a boyishly low voice, she asked, "What brings you to this quiet corner of the world, Mr. William?" She felt entitled to ask; had he not quizzed her? Apparently this was how males behaved when they encountered one another at inns.

The gentleman gave her a merry glance. "Sir, I am an author! That is to say, specifically, a poet! I seek this sylvan retreat to court the Muse!" He paused, grinning. "Also I am rusticating for the purpose of discouraging my creditors. You may say I am trying to outrun the tipstaffs! Behold me all aquake!"

Joining in his laughter, Andrea yet felt a little disgust for the theatricality of his manner. This colored her voice with a hint of censure as she replied, "One cannot feel too much compassion for so cheerful an exile. But if you are so lacking in funds, do you not fear that you may not be able to pay the charges at this inn?"

"But it is the *smaller* of the two inns," explained the man grinning. "Therefore I judge it to be the less expensive."

Andrea puzzled for a moment over this piece of irrationality. Then she raised her eyes and caught the twinkle in Mr. William's. "You are making a joke," she said.

Mr. William shouted with laughter. "What a sober youth it is! The life of a scholar will suit you. That is, if you are always this calmly rational?"

"I try to be so, sir," responded poor Andrea, not sure she was presenting the proper image for a young man.

"It is true that powerful emotions—hatred, love, grief, fear—can be debilitating. But have you never yourself dreaded a rival or mourned a fair lady?"

"Never," said Andrea, taking another slice of roast beef and a second generous wedge of Yorkshire pudding.

The man regarded her with admiration. "It is obvious I am in the presence of a sensible man," he said. "Do you always break your fast so enthusiastically?"

"This is my dinner, sir," said Andrea, wiping the gravy from her plate with a crust of new-baked bread. "I had breakfast a long time ago."

William chuckled. "If it is your habit to stuff your gut so greedily, my boy, you'll soon have a belly as big as the Regent's."

Before she could prevent herself, Andrea lifted a shocked and minatory glance. Gentlemen did not speak thus crudely in the presence of a lady! Then with a sudden lurch of fear, she recalled that she was not a *jeune fille bien gardée,* but a male student traveling independently. Such a one would hardly take umbrage at a few coarse phrases. She forced a smile and shrugged as she patted her flat stomach.

William had taken her momentary bristle of hackles as a response to his teasing. "Never fear, youngling, you'll grow up to be a man before your mother."

Since this incomprehensible comment was accompanied by a smile, it must be a male joke of some sort. Andrea smiled politely and changed the subject. "What do you think of Kyle Village—or have you just arrived?"

"Oh, no, this is my second visit. I went south to scout out the land, see if my creditors were still humming. In fact, I had hoped that I might be able to remain there, but the wasps still buzz and I—er—loped off. Of course, my creditors alone might not have routed me, but there was a certain lady who became too serious—" he leered complacently. "You understand me, Bart, I'm sure."

"Perfectly," said Andrea, not really understanding anything except that she found this man rather silly. First he boasted of not paying his debts, then of running away from a lady who took him seriously. Still, he seemed disposed to be friendly, and perhaps, since he had been here in Kyle Village for some time, he might be able to furnish information she needed. With this thought in mind, she began, casually, as they waited for the dessert to be brought in,

"What do you know of the lord of Kyle? I hear he has been recently widowed."

William's response to this was surprising. He glanced around quickly to assure himself that no member of the inn staff was within hearing distance. "You'll be well advised to ask no questions about his lordship, boy, nor to let any of the loyal serfs hereabouts suspect you of prying."

"Prying!" The suddenness of the attack startled the girl. " 'Twas the merest commonplace— idle curiosity about the local lord—"

"There is no such thing as commonplace with these people where their liege is concerned. 'Tis a feudal enclave, I tell you! The clansmen have a fanatical devotion to their laird! Everything we do is reported to Milord's bailiff. Kyle has its own army, its special justice, even its dungeons. Lord Dominic Justin is as absolute a monarch as ever Europe knew!" His dark eyes were narrow with anger.

"Why, sir, here's heat!" commented Andrea. "Have you run afoul of Milord's justice?"

William sat back and sipped his ale. Then, grinning wryly, he said in a lowered tone, "I'll admit I've had a brush or two with Milord's private army. I was wandering through the woods one fine evening, seeking inspiration for a poem, when I was roughly accosted by two burly fellows and urged to give a reason for trespassing upon Milord's sacred territory. I escaped a drubbing by the exercise of some fast talk and an even faster pair of heels when I had them off guard. Then, upon another occasion, I made myself a thought too friendly to a buxom Amaryllis, and her doughty swain nearly broke my jaw for me." He sighed and rubbed his chin ruefully. "I watch my tongue *and* my comings and goings these days."

Andrea, meeting those bright black eyes, had the strong notion that, were she the doughty swain, she would guard her back and walk warily. For the genial Mr. William, in those moments of recollection, was not the posturing poet he seemed eager to represent.

Later on that evening, when the young moon rose over the trees, Andrea swung wide her dormer window and leaned on the sill. The evening was warm, and delicately scented by the flowers and herbs in the garden below. She had hung her new blue coat carefully over a chair-back, removed her boots and donned the tiger slippers thankfully. Feeling very comfortable, she rested her elbows on the wide sill and looked into the night. The moonlight bathed her face and silvered the bright gold of her hair.

She heard a little gasp of pleasure from the dark garden below her, followed by a throaty laugh. She scanned the darkness involuntarily, then chided herself. Not at all the thing to spy on young lovers! Still, she found it impossible to avoid looking. She made out a girl sitting alone on a bench. The girl in turn was staring up at

Andrea. When she realized she had been noticed, she rose and moved forward.

"Would you not like to come down and enjoy the sweet night air with me, young sir?" There was another low, seductive laugh, then the girl continued, "Or perhaps your honor would rather I came up?"

"Another time," gulped Andrea, closing the window abruptly. Was this Mr. William's Amaryllis? "Really," she thought, as she checked to make sure her door was locked before she undressed for bed, "these Scottish girls behave very boldly!"

At that point, hanging up the new breeches, she was reminded of her own behavior during this last week, and went to bed smiling ruefully.

The following day she tried to get information from the maid who served her breakfast, but although the wench seemed eager to flirt, she became singularly uncommunicative when asked direct questions about the Castle and its master. Fearing to arouse undue curiosity about her own background and person, Andrea fell silent. It was becoming obvious that all Milord's tenants had a healthy respect for Milord's privacy!

She rode further afield the next day, spying out the terrain for Pola's ride. Then that evening, after supper, when the lingering light of the northern sunset turned the rich fields and distant mountains to gold, Andrea wandered out of the inn to stroll once more through the quiet village. Everyone seemed to be at supper.

The fields and streets were equally deserted. She admired again the neat cottages and the well-kept gardens. The cascading stream turned the great mill wheel lazily, making a pleasant sound of splashing waters. All was bounteous, all was orderly. At least the master of Kyle was a good landlord, and his domain was more prosperous than that of Castle Wasylyk. Frowning, Andrea considered the villagers she had met. They seemed cheerful, if reserved toward strangers, and there was never a hint of the harsh surveillance and the iron control Mr. William had described.

Yet Andrea was to encounter a painful proof of the correctness of that gentleman's advice. She decided to try once more to get information by listening to conversations in a taproom—an exercise she had so far eschewed. Ruthlessly she put down her growing distaste at her role of spy upon Lord Justin. She hesitated outside the taproom of the larger inn, telling herself that if her father and sister had indeed been murdered as she suspected, it was her duty to bring their killer to justice. She strolled into the tavern, trying hard for nonchalance.

No one took any notice of her. She spotted Mr. William seated at a table with a convivial group, but avoided looking at him after the first glance. She went over to the bar and asked for a glass of ale.

One of the patrons said slyly, "Wouldn't that be a glass of milk, Tom?"

The barman ignored the remark, but a couple

of other men chuckled. Andrea took a gold coin out of her pocket and pushed it toward the barman. As she was picking up her change, she asked the man next to her, the one who had mentioned milk, "Does Lord Justin ever come to this tavern?"

"Better ask Tom," the fellow replied. "Ah'm a stranger here mahsel'." There was another general laugh, this time louder.

Tom was frowning as he polished the bar with a clean cloth. "Will that be all, young sir? Or will there be something to eat?" and he gestured toward a small empty table near the bar.

Thinking the man might be more forthcoming if she could speak to him in the relative privacy of the empty table, Andrea nodded and went to seat herself. Tom followed her part way, then went on to the kitchen and sent out a barmaid.

"And what will your honor have to eat and drink?" this girl enquired, with a saucy look and one plump hip outthrust.

Andrea ordered some bread and butter.

The girl looked disappointed. "Cheese, too?" she suggested. "It's awfu' gude wi' the baps."

Andrea, feeling helpless, agreed to the suggestion and waited impatiently for the return of the girl. On her way back to the table, the maid collected the ale Andrea had left on the bar, and placed it down with the bread and cheese. "Now enjoy the gude fude," she said. Andrea pulled another gold coin out and offered it to her.

"It was very sad about the young Lady Justin," she offered. I suppose you had hardly time to get to know her—"

"Och, now, what would I be doin' wi' such a fine leddy? 'Tis more interested in the menfolk, I am," teased the girl. "Would yer honor be wantin' company the nicht?"

Ye gods! thought Andrea, rising hurriedly. Was the whole female servant staff of these inns crazed for a male? She did not wait for her change, but went out of the inn. As she walked away she heard laughter. She had no doubt her enquiries would be reported, but she had got little good of them.

Disgruntled by her failures to secure information, Andrea decided to take advantage of the long northern twilight and try a minor penetration into Lord Justin's extensive acres. She slipped across the meadows and into the woods, and, finding a well-marked path, climbed up the hill to where an open glade presented a clear view of the lofty castle walls looming against the western skies. Andrea drew a breath of surprise and appreciation. The lord of Kyle ruled a fair stronghold. There were battlements and parapets, and a round, slit-windowed keep which looked suspiciously like a dungeon to Andrea. From the topmost tower flew Milord's banner, a black sword upon a field of scarlet.

"Medieval," sniffed Andrea, but found her Wasylyk blood stirred by the challenging male arrogance of the standard. She decided to make the unplanned reconnoiter useful by sketching the castle and its environs. Moving out into the glade to get the last of the daylight, and propping her knee on a rock, she pulled from her capacious pocket the notebook without which she never ventured forth from the inn, found a blank page, and began to draw the outline of the magnificent structure, particularly noting entrances and ways of approach.

Suddenly a very heavy hand fell on her shoulder. Almost staggered by the blow, the girl turned to face her attacker. It was one of a pair of burly fellows dressed in neat leather jerkins and high boots. Each one carried a stout staff. Andrea could only give thanks that the blow had been dealt by hand.

"And what might ye be doin', young sir?"

"I am sketching the castle," Andrea managed to reply in her deep boy's-voice.

"For what purpose?" continued the remorseless inquisition.

Andrea thought fast. " 'Tis to be the frontispiece of my book upon the herbs of this region, my man," she said courteously, resisting the impulse to rub the aching shoulder. "And what may be your purpose in accosting me?"

Both sets of bushy eyebrows rose in incredulity. "Our purpose, says you?" The older man, who had not yet spoken, now gave voice. "Our purpose, bantling, is to patrol Lord Justin's demesne and keep the peace."

Andrea managed a smile. "I assure you, my good man, I am a very peaceful citizen."

It seemed that would not do. "And what would

be your business in this village, young sir? For the host of The Stag tells us you are here for a lengthy visit. What is your business here?"

Andrea, daughter of a long line of Polish counts, felt her anger rise. "I am here upon my own legitimate affairs, fellow, which happen to be personal. I pay my bills and create neither riot nor rumpus. I resent your officiousness!"

"Do ye now?" mused the older man. "Mayhap ye'd better come away with us to the bailiff and explain that same private affairs."

Scrambling to preserve her dignity, Andrea said coldly, "I shall be pleased to receive your bailiff at The Stag. You may tell him I shall await his attendance upon me there. My name is Bartholomew."

"Ah, that'll be the young colleger," nodded the older man. "Terrible resty, these young collegers," he advised the younger patrolman, and they both laughed.

Andrea's cheek burned with rage. Child-woman though she was, quiet and cloistered as she had lived in school and in her father's various residences, she had still the blood of a dozen generations of soldiers burning in her veins.

"You are pleased to be insolent, sirrah! You will bring me this bailiff at once! I wish to report your behavior."

There was an arrested expression on the two hard faces. They had been born and bred in their lord's service, and their fathers before them, and they recognized the authentic voice of the master. Perchance this youngling was a noble sprout, and had authority behind him. The older man was ready to back off, now, but the younger felt an overwhelming need to deflate this banty in the town-cut clothes. He reached out one huge paw, gathered a thick fold of cloth at the nape of the little man's neck, and lifted him off his feet, dangling him ludicrously at arm's length.

It was too much. Blinded by fury, Andrea struck out with open palm and slapped her attacker across the face. The man's countenance swelled and darkened with anger. Grinding out an oath, he lifted his other huge fist to avenge the blow.

A cold voice rang at their shoulders.

"What is the meaning of this, Ben?"

Both guards turned to confront a magnificent figure mounted on a huge black stallion. The older yeoman touched his cap.

"We were takin' the muster of strangers in the village, Milord," he said humbly. "We learned that this young sprig had been askin' questions, and had vanished. We found him."

He and Lord Justin turned their eyes to the ludicrous tableau before them. Ben, the younger guard, was frozen into position by the unexpected appearance of his master, and stood stupidly holding the slender figure of the trespasser by the loose material at the back of the coat. The youth's face was a study in rage and embarrassment as he dangled from that mighty paw.

Unexpectedly the two older men broke into short, quickly stifled laughter.

"I think you may safely release the gentleman," advised Lord Justin.

Grinning nervously, Ben set Andrea carefully back on her feet. From scarlet her face had drained to white. She glared up at Lord Justin, high on his monstrous horse. Although he was attired in faultless buckskins and an elegant riding coat, he gave the impression of wearing armor. Andrea was conscious of such a chaos of conflicting emotions that she was nearly strangled. So this man—larger than life and devastatingly handsome—was the lord of Kyle! Pola's husband—perhaps Pola's murderer! It was not so strange that she hardly remembered him. She had seen him so briefly in the candle-lit gloom of the ballroom and in the dining room. More, she had had to watch him through the stifling folds of that ridiculous veil. It was obvious he did not recall ever seeing her before, as in truth he had not actually done. She stared with unconscious insolence into his tanned, arrogant face, and was surprised to find it beautiful. She must not reveal to those fierce, probing, iron-gray eyes that she was a woman; nor must he guess her true name or her errand here. Oh, how she would love to challenge him at this instant, and run him through with her rapier! She ground her teeth with the desperation of her unobtainable wish.

On his part, Lord Dominic Justin found himself moved by the pale, anguished face. He realized that the boy was bitterly humiliated and raging to claim revenge. Quietly he said,

"You are trespassing, you know."

"I was not aware that Milord of Kyle owned the whole countryside," flashed Andrea.

This open defiance was too much for Ben. "Keep a civil tongue in yer head, spriggins!" he growled, then faced the man on the horse to explain his behavior. "We sees him spyin' out the land, Milord." He picked up the notebook which had dropped to the ground during the brief scuffle.

Lord Justin held out his hand and Ben placed the book in it.

Andrea gasped with outrage. "I believe that is my property, sir. You have no right—"

"Silence! If you remain in this vicinity, you will do well to remember that I have every right to do whatever I wish. I am the master here." Ignoring her mutterings, he coolly opened the book and flipped a few of the pages. A partly-dried wild rose fluttered out and drifted to the ground. Lord Justin glanced at Ben. "This seems harmless enough—a simple collection of weeds and sketches of weeds. With notes written in a very pretty hand," he smiled slightly into the blazing eyes of Andrea.

Before the girl could answer, Ben spoke again. " 'Twas a map o' the castle, Milord," he persisted. "Matt an' me saw it—drawn devilish plain."

Frowning, Lord Justin flipped the pages until he found the sketch Andrea had made. He raised one eyebrow at the girl, who was by now shaking with anger. "Well? May I know the purpose of this remarkably detailed sketch?"

"I had thought," said Andrea between her teeth, "to use it as a pretty bit of local color to illustrate my report."

Milord's face hardened. "Report?"

"Remember your story," the girl cautioned herself. "You could destroy all by an excess of sensibility now!" Attempting to compose her features, she said in a low voice, "I am a botanist, a scholar preparing a report for my tutor at Oxford." *Toujours l'audace!* she encouraged herself, and head high, held out one slender hand. "May I have my notebook, please?"

Lord Justin continued to scrutinize her. "You are the student who is staying at The Stag?" He examined her boldly, from the neatly-brushed cap of golden curls to the small, well-shod feet. "Your guardians should not have let you roam abroad without your tutor."

Ben guffawed again.

Andrea continued to hold her head high on the slender throat. "It is true that I am a scholar, sir. Apparently that is a species unknown in this vicinity."

Unexpectedly Milord chuckled. "A little bantam cock, is it? Well, that's a welcome relief from your fellow guest at The Stag, who skulks about by night and makes himself overly-familiar with the girls in the village. Does he too claim to be a scholar?"

"He is a poet, sir!" announced Andrea, more

75

annoyed by his teasing than his anger. Was there to be no end to this catechism?

Milord was regarding her arrogantly. "You are a friend of his?"

"A new friend. I have just arrived recently."

"Four days ago, in fact," said Milord.

Andrea couldn't resist the opportunity. "It seems there is, in truth, spying going on in your demesne, Milord," she said pertly. "You are to be congratulated on your—intelligencers," she gave the fuming Ben a scornful glance.

"Don't push your luck, bantling," warned Lord Justin. "And don't let my men catch you on my property again, or they'll teach you something you didn't learn at Oxford."

Ben and Matt received this with great amusement. Andrea knew that she should lower her crest and leave at once, while Milord yet held his servants on rein, but the insults of this self-important man had set her teeth on edge. Unwisely she taunted, "Have you been able to mark the boundaries of your *property* well enough for a literate man to read them? Or do you rely on traps and bullies?"

The guards gasped at this effrontery, and Milord's eyes, hard and gray as metal, narrowed.

"It would be well for you if you brought your spectacles, scholar!"

"I'll be more like to bring my sword!" flamed the girl, carried away by the argument and by her sense of injustice.

There was a sudden silence. Andrea realized,

too late, that she had inadvertently given a male signal of aggression, and her blood ran cold. Count Vladimir had permitted Pola and her to fence with him, and Andrea, happy to share any exercise with her father, had practiced as often as he would permit during her holidays at the castle, but she knew positively that this man was in a class she could never hope to enter. He was staring at her with a perfectly expressionless face.

"You bear a sword?" he asked coldly.

"I have one, Milord—but it is not with me."

"Fortunate for you."

Really, the man was insufferable!

The grimmest smile she had ever seen touched the well-shaped lips. "If you come this way again, sir, you had better wear it," Lord Justin advised.

Andrea, shocked out of her anger and thankful to be escaping so easily, turned without a farewell to this infuriating tyrant. Ben thrust his foot out as she moved, and she tripped over it and went sprawling on the ground. Ben guffawed as the slight figure picked itself up slowly. Face white with humiliation, she stared into Milord's face, ignoring his guard entirely. "That was inexcusable!" she stated clearly. "I demand an apology—or a meeting!"

At that moment she would most eagerly have crossed swords with the devil himself, to say nothing of the lord of Kyle Castle. Both henchmen were silent now, and withdrew a few paces from Andrea. The girl, moved out of all reason by anger and embarrassment, went on, "You will please to name your friends, Milord. I imagine Mr. William will second me."

Lord Justin stared at her for a long moment and then seemed to come to a decision. "It was inexcusable. I offer my apologies." Then, as his henchmen gaped at him, he said softly, "I do not murder children."

"Only women?" Andrea sneered, sotto voce, but Lord Justin heard her. Putting his horse forward in a lightning thrust, he bent and struck her with his riding whip. Her own quick reflex in throwing up her arm saved her face from the smashing blow, but the pain in her arm was so severe that she fell to her knees.

"You are fortunate indeed, you young blackguard," Milord's voice came to her through a haze of pain. "It is not long since a master of Kyle would have had your tongue out for that piece of scurrility. Go while you can still walk."

He turned his great horse and cantered off along the path toward the castle. After a few minutes, the pain subsided enough for Andrea to scramble to her feet and stagger down the track toward the village. She was conscious of the two yeomen coming along behind her, but she did not address them, nor did they offer to speak to her. It was full dark by the time she came back to The Stag. There were lamps lighted in the inn, and the sound of voices raised in amicable argument. Andrea crept up the stairs to her bedroom and shut and locked the door.

Her first meeting with the lord of Kyle on his

own turf had not been auspicious. It now remained to be seen if he would have her driven out of the village. Wearily she bathed the swelling arm in cold water from her pitcher, and then wet a towel and held that to it. Finally she undressed slowly and crept into bed.

Chapter Seven

AFTER A TROUBLED, PAIN-FILLED NIGHT, Andrea awoke to bright sunlight streaming into the bedroom. She lay for a time, trying to compel herself to rise and continue the secret campaign against Lord Justin. Her upper arm was swollen and deeply bruised, but the shock of her injuries went deeper than the physical. In all her seventeen years, Andrea had never known the impact of physical brutality, and though she had felt lonely and rejected often, she had always been treated with courtesy and respect by everyone but Pola. The treatment she had received at the hands of Lord Justin and his men was a stunning surprise.

To do them justice, they had not known she was a girl. She told herself to remember that. But she had also to realize that if she persisted in her plan to unmask the lord of Kyle, she would hazard the risk of being treated far more harshly than she had already been. She paused, struck by the memory of Milord's apology. She was constrained to admit that he had offered formal regrets for his henchman's action in tripping her as she prepared to leave. She knew she had only herself to thank for that final blow. She had accused Lord Justin of murder! In the clear light of dawn she shuddered at her irresponsible behavior—"scurrilous blackguard" was his evaluation of her—and wondered that, in the circumstances, he had let her off so lightly.

These logical doubts Andrea swept aside by recalling the simple facts of the situation: a sister dead within a month of her marriage, a father mysteriously struck down, and this to be laid at the door of Lord Dominic Justin. Her resolve to continue with her plan hardened as she recalled her humiliation, his odious laughter, his open threats to her life. But caution dictated that her next attack be something more subtle than a frontal, physical one. It was time for her impersonation of Pola's ghost.

As she dragged herself out of bed, she wondered if she would have the strength to carry out her plan. She intended to dress herself in the flowing pale green garment and veil she had worn as a bridesmaid, and ride tonight somewhere where she would be seen. The presence of a ghostlike figure would surely be widely reported and commented upon. In the light of her new knowledge of Milord's quality and temper, however, she had better be sure she didn't ride into one of his patrols and find herself hauled ignominiously before him to her unmasking!

Still pondering the problem, Andrea washed and then clumsily dressed herself in her masculine costume. She really had no appetite, and the pain in her arm sent waves of nausea through her, but she felt she must at least put in an appearance in the dining room of the inn. She found Mr. William there before her, moodily sipping at some concoction in a large mug. He gave her a morose greeting.

"Are you not feeling quite the thing this morning?" Andrea enquired politely.

"I was a great deal too well to do last night," admitted William. "Cursed powerful potations our host brews up. I should have known better." He shuddered. "I think it an object with these rustics to put us under the table."

Andrea inferred that he had drunk too much and was feeling vilely unwell, but had no sympathy to spare for such stupidity. She herself, however, pecked languidly at the enormous meal the giggling Freda served. Her unusual restraint attracted her companion's interest.

"Feeling a bit queazy yourself, Bart?" he asked. "I saw you last night at the Arms, but missed you later in the taproom here. Have you found a better grog shop?"

Some measure of openness seemed essential, if she were not to set herself up as a figure of mystery, the last thing she wished to suggest. Andrea therefore shrugged ruefully and indicated her arm. "I had a nasty fall last night. I was strolling about, enjoying the peace and beauty of the evening, and decided to walk up through the woods below the Castle. I had a little—er—discussion with two of Milord's guards."

William stared at her with raised eyebrows. "You are a fool, of course. You could have been killed. The master of Kyle is ruthless, and his henchmen are a gang of bullies. Whatever can have possessed you to wander into the lion's den?"

"I am not accustomed to being hampered in my movements. It did not occur to me that anyone would object to my strolling through the woods on a pleasant evening. The moon was rising as I came back to the inn."

Her disgression was ignored. "You mean you actually haven't heard about the local tragedy? Milord's wife had a very peculiar accident just a few weeks ago, which resulted in her death. Tempers are short and suspicion is widespread. Rather a nasty little situation to walk into, Bart."

"But surely I have nothing to say to any of that!" offered Andrea, very casually. "I only arrived a few days ago."

"If you think that exonerates you in the eyes of these rustics, you are lamentably ignorant. I've been the target of a great deal of suspicion," William added grimly, "on the basis, one presumes, that a poet is a loose, idle and disorderly person, without visible means of support, and unable to give a satisfactory account of himself."

Andrea found herself smiling at the flowing periods. "Oh, no! Are you really? Loose, idle and disorderly, or whatever?"

William put on an affronted stare. "That, my

young scamp, is the legal definition of a vagabond, and presumably, to these peasants, a poet
fits neatly into the category. Your own Shake-
speare and his fellow actors were so described."

"I see I have been moving in some pretty
dangerous company," Andrea chuckled.

The dining room door opened and Applegate
entered, bearing a small package and a newly-
respectful demeanor.

"This has just come for you, young sir. From
the Castle." He placed the package into Andrea's
hands. "Message from his lordship was, 'De-
liver this into the hands of Mr. Bartholomew,
and bid him farewell.' Are you leaving us, then,
sir?"

"Thank you," stammered Andrea, staring from
the host's face to the small, heavy parcel. "No, I
have no plans to remove at once," she added. "I
am very satisfied with this inn."

Since she did not seem about to offer further
comment or to open the parcel immediately,
Applegate retreated reluctantly and closed the
door after him.

Andrea raised her eyes and encountered a
coolly-assessing glance from her companion. "So?
A present from the great man himself?"

Flushing, Andrea made haste to open the
package. Inside was her notebook, which had
fallen to the ground during Milord's final attack. Unable to meet William's quizzical stare,
she busied herself leafing through the pages.
Missing was the dried, battered rose which had
been dislodged during Justin's disdainful in-

vestigation. The page near the end, where she had drawn the Castle, was also missing, but there was a note in its place. Without offering any apology, she opened it and read the contents, written in a bold, slashing hand remarkably suited to its author.

Lord Justin had written:

> Herewith your property returned in good order, except for one battered specimen which I am sure you can replace without too much trouble. Other things, however, are not so easily restored.
> When you have picked your rose, I suggest that you return with all haste to those academic groves which I am sure you grace so fittingly. The wind blows cold and harsh in the real world, scholar. *Verbum sap.*
>
> Justin

Andrea raised a face red with anger. "Insufferable! He has ordered me to leave, with threats!"

"Shall you do so?" William's eyes were sparkling with amusement, yet beneath the laughter there was speculation. "I had not realized you were such a fire-eater! Whatever did you do, on your simple moonlit stroll, to bring down the wrath of Jove upon your curly head?"

"I called him a murderer," admitted Andrea, somewhat rashly.

There was a pregnant silence. She raised her eyes to catch a look of almost painful attention on Mr. William's swarthy, handsome countenance. "Phew!" breathed that gentleman softly. "You must be under the direct protection of a guardian angel! You tell me that you accused the master of Kyle of *that* . . . and live to tell the tale?"

"Well, I had challenged him to a duel, but he apologized instead, and I do think I might have gotten off with only my pride ruffled if I hadn't made that final remark," Andrea confessed, a little shame-faced.

William was regarding her with incredulity tinged by amusement. "Heaven protects fools," he murmured, "*You* challenged him and *he* apologized?" The man shook his head. "I wonder if you will condescend to relate to me the full tale of your moonlight walk? I assure you, it is not idle curiosity on my part."

"Not? Then why do you wish to hear the story?" countered Andrea, some faint warnings of caution struggling with hurt pride and anger.

"Perhaps I might be of assistance to you, Bart, if I knew the whole," coaxed William, grinning. "Don't tell me you're going to be selfish and keep this marvelous adventure to yourself?"

Andrea's inclination was to enlist the help of this very personable man. Still, she warned herself, the task which she had set herself was of such a dangerous nature that it must be cloaked in secrecy if it were to have any chance of succeeding. No, charming as she was beginning to find her fellow guest, she must never lose sight of her objective. While these ideas were racing through her mind, William bent over and plucked the note from her fingers. Ignoring her look of outrage, he scanned the single sheet rapidly.

Andrea snatched the page back. Any impulse to confide in this impudent fellow was banished. She rejected his playful efforts to apologize and almost sullenly ignored him for the rest of the meal. Immediately afterward she bundled up the wrappings, her book, and the note, and retired to her bedroom. There, behind a locked door, she examined what Lord Justin had sent. Her eye was caught by two tiny paper packets which she had not previously noted among the heavy wrapping paper. On one of them she perceived more of Milord's distinctive script. "To be taken for the relief of pain."

She sat down slowly and stared at the medicine in her hands. He noticed everything, this devil of a Scottish aristocrat! He had remembered the blow of his crop, and had known how it would hurt. But why had he bothered to send medicine? That was not in character! Could it be poison? Or even some drug which would render her helpless or nauseated? A fine jest, that! She could imagine Ben's coarse laughter. With an angry gesture that ignored her bruised arm, she tossed the packets onto her bed. An agonizing twinge immediately reminded her. Hastily she stripped off her coat and shirt and considered the swollen, purple and black-bruised member. Her glance strayed to the medicine. He had let the scurrilous blackguard suffer all night, to teach him a lesson, but in the morning came the relief. A merciful gesture? Slowly Andrea went to the washstand, poured water from the pitcher into a cup, and emptied one of the powders into it. She lifted the cup to her lips, hesitated, then drained it. Then she lay down on her bed to await the results. If I die, she thought grimly, he'll have another murder to explain!

The next she knew, she was awakened by a knocking on the door.

"Who is it?" she called out drowsily.

"The maid, sir. May I tidy up the room?"

With a hasty glance at her unclothed torso, Andrea said sharply, "I'm dressing for dinner."

Ye gods, what time was it? "How long did I sleep?" The sun was slanting across the trees outside her window. Late afternoon, then. She felt remarkably rested and restored, and her arm, when she flexed it gingerly, did not hurt quite so badly. No poison, then, she thought. To the girl, giggling outside her door in a manner which Andrea considered to be decidedly silly, she called out, "I'll be out of here in ten minutes. Come back later."

After she had heard the retreating footsteps, she placed Lord Justin's note carefully inside her coat and left the second packet of medicine on the night stand. She washed awkwardly, dressed herself in a fresh binder and shirt, and eased into her coat. Thank God it was not fashionably skin-tight! Taking the wooden-handled brush, she tried to bring her unruly curls into some semblance of masculine neatness. Then she went down to the dining room. The table was set, and some of the salads and cold dishes and breads were already in place. As she entered, she observed that Applegate and William were engaged in a serious conversation by the window. Both men looked up as she entered.

"Ah, Mr. Bartholomew," her host greeted her. "I was just asking Mr. William if he knew when you planned to leave us."

"I have no intention of leaving before the time I set," replied Andrea sternly.

"But his lordship's message—"

"I am sure you misunderstood it," replied Andrea carelessly. "Is supper to be served at once? I am sharp-set after my nap."

Looking uncomfortable, Applegate hurried from the room.

William regarded the slim figure curiously. "You surprise me, young Bart. I suppose you do realize that you have just defied the great man? Who are you, anyway? The cub of some noble house? What are you doing in this medieval corner of the island?"

Andrea raised her eyebrows but did not vouchsafe a reply. After watching her for a long moment, William continued in quite a different tone, "I wish you would confide in me. It might be that I could help you."

"With what?"

"Whatever it is that brings a child like you to this place. Oh, don't ruffle your feathers at me! And don't tell me about Oxford and the great botanical report. I wasn't born yesterday, nor was Lord Justin, if you've any doubts about the matter."

"I think men of your age and Lord Justin's get very odd ideas sometimes," said Andrea outrageously. She was delighted to observe that Mr. William, who could not have been older than seven or eight and twenty, turned a very unattractive shade of puce at the jibe.

"What's that supposed to mean, you young whipper-snapper?" he snarled, his conciliating attitude quite set aside.

Andrea grinned. "I thought that fine avuncular manner sat a little loosely on your shoulders," she said. "Do you play piquet?"

"Yes, but I'm not going to. Did you really challenge Milord to a duel?"

"Yes, I'm afraid so. It was a thought rash of me, since I have only had about a dozen lessons, over the years. And I've never fought with the buttons off."

"My God!" William exhaled in exasperation. "You are mad! If you can't fight, then why did you issue a challenge? He would have killed you!"

"I was very angry," said Andrea quietly.

"You would have been very dead," her companion said grimly. "As with everything else, Lord Dominic Justin is a nonpareil with the sword. What I can't understand is his forbearance. You've insulted him beyond forgiveness, disobeyed his command to get out of his bailiwick, challenged him to a duel—"

"He said he didn't murder children."

William drew a sharp breath. Then, "You are suggesting he has a sense of compunction?"

"I'm suggesting nothing, and I'm getting bored with this conversation," announced Andrea, seating herself at the table.

William glared at her with loathing. "You are a brat," he said. "Rude, disagreeable, impertinent—I've a good mind to turn you over my knee."

"Try it and I will—I will bite you to the bone," Andrea offered steadily.

"Hellhound!" William glared at her a moment longer and then flung himself down at the table.

The excellent meal was eaten in a cold silence. When it was over, Andrea rose to go to her room.

"How about the piquet?" asked William, who seemed to have recovered his equanimity.

"I find I do not wish to play with you after all," Andrea said, and went out of the room, leaving William muttering about barbarians, hellhounds, and spoiled brats.

In her bedroom, the girl stood looking out the window, carefully scanning as much of the village as she could see from that vantage point. The ghost of Pola could parade down that broad main street, but what if some farmer returning late from the tavern, or worse, one of Milord's patrols, should run into her? Ideally, Andrea decided, she would have to show herself from a place clearly visible to as many persons as possible, yet not easily approached for investigation.

Then, as though it had been waiting for her need, a perfect scheme rose in her imagination. She checked the details rapidly. If, just after moon-rise, a ghostly figure showed itself upon the cliff-top above the mill, attracted attention in some dramatic way, and then, while the villagers were approaching to investigate, mounted a horse neatly hobbled just beneath the rim of the cliff at the rear and rode away toward the ocean, the ghost would then be in a position to ride again along the sand to the westward, or ocean, side of the Castle while its guards were off-balance with the first appearance.

That was the rub. In her botanical wanderings Andrea had marked all the ways, including cart-tracks and footpaths, which led to the Castle. She had even wandered along that path, on the cliff above the ocean, from which Pola was said to have been thrown by the rogue horse. She was sure she could get from the mill to the ocean cliffs quickly—*but what if she ran into one of Milord's patrols?* She had had phenomenal luck, avoiding them every time but the one disastrous encounter, but would the luck hold? Surely they were on the alert since her encounter with Milord?

Opening her trunk, she took from the bottom her one weapon, her father's ceremonial dagger. He had been wont to wear it with his court dress. The hilt and sheath flashed and sparkled with inset gems, but the blade was finest Toledo-forged. Andrea held the small, deadly thing. It bore the crest of her house. If Justin ever saw it, he would know at once whence the attack came. But that would be simple justice, would it not? She frowned. Did she mean to plunge her father's dagger into the man's breast? With a shiver, she knew she could not do so. He had spared her; she would spare his life, but she would force him to admit what he had done. Her own blood should be crying out for vengeance upon the murderer of a father and sister! But she could not envision herself striking the essential blow. Sighing, she placed the dagger back in the trunk and began to take off her clothes.

Chapter Eight

ANDREA DONNED A PAIR of her old slim
black riding breeches and black riding boots.
Then she pulled a plain white shirt over her
binding cloth, and sat down at the table where
she had propped up a mirror between the two
candles the room boasted. Opening a tin box,
she covered her face with the white paste it
contained. The resultant mask looked nothing
like Andrea, or indeed, any other human vis-
age, and she regarded it with satisfaction. Next
she took out a small pot of black and smoothed
it around her eyes. This made so ghastly an
effect that the girl was delighted. She debated
on coloring her mouth with the red paste which
was the third and last of the cosmetic ointments
she had purchased from the apothecary shop.
On second thought she judged that the black
and white mask was more ghost-like.

Next she pulled the pale green gown with its
layers of soft floating material. This was full
and quite long enough to hide her breeches and
boots. The long veil fell mysteriously around
her, blurring her outline. She caught up her
discarded clothing, put it away neatly, hid the
tin box in the bottom of her trunk, locked it,

and put her tinderbox and flints in a canvas bag along with ten guineas. In case something should go awry, and flight become necessary, she wanted to have money with her.

Now, what she considered to be the most dangerous part of her plan was at hand. She must get safely out of the inn to the stables, and get away without being seen. She took a final look around the room, moved hastily to pull back the counterpane and top sheet as though someone had hastily risen from sleep, and then snuffed both candles. She swept the voluminous folds of her draperies into her arms and tied the bag with the money and tools to her belt. Then she opened the door of her room and peered into the hallway. The doors of the other three bed-rooms were closed. The hall was dark, but some light reflected up the stairwell from the common room below. From a distance came the low rumble of voices of men. Andrea locked her door from the outside and crept toward the narrow back stairs which led down to the kitchen. Heavy smells of cooking rose around her as she felt her way down the stairs. In the kitchen itself, all was dark. She knew the back door was to the right of the big window ahead of her. She moved slowly around the kitchen table. Then she was at the back door and fumbling for the handle. To her surprise, the knob turned easily. She swung the door inward and slipped past it into the inn yard.

Here the cobblestones were treacherous under

her feet, and she kept to the shadow of the building as she made her way around to the stable. A single lantern burned near the open door, hanging from a great iron hook. As far as Andrea could see, the ostlers and stableboys were asleep or away drinking or wenching. Carefully she donned the veil, having first made sure of her direction. She went into the stable slowly, her feet silent on the straw.

From close to her came a muted squawk, then a thud. She swung around to see the body of one of the stableboys stretched out on the ground. Congratulating herself upon the success of her disguise, she hurriedly saddled her horse, hoping that the boy's faint would hold him till she was gone. As she was preparing to mount, it occurred to her that an investigation would reveal that Mr. Bartholomew's was the only horse missing from the stables. Conscientiously she led all the horses to the door and drove them out with a sharp slap on the rump. They wouldn't go far, probably, but in the confusion she hoped to create, it might be thought that her horse had gone further. Catching it would give her an excuse for being away from the inn. Much pleased with her clever thinking, the girl caught up an armful of straw under her veil. She mounted without too much difficulty, and disposed her veil and skirts over the saddle. She had no idea how she looked, but the stableboy's faint had assured her that her disguise was effective. On her way out of the stable she extinguished the lantern.

The diversion with the horses proved almost too effective. As she rode quietly down the road, keeping to the soft earth by the verge to muffle the sound of the horse's hooves, she heard a shout from behind her, at the inn. Bad luck! The stableboy had come to his senses and discovered the absence of the horses. There was not a moment to be lost! As shouts of enquiry from the inn answered the stableboy's appeals, Andrea directed Boyo into the track which led past the mill and up to the crag behind it. Boyo threaded his way neatly in the dim light furnished by the rising moon. He was a lovely animal, and Andrea loved and trusted him. Many times on the long, exhausting ride from London she'd beguiled the weary hours conversing with him, sharing her hopes and angers and fears; she felt the horse knew her as no one else did. She had schooled him in dressage, teaching him all the Cossack officer had taught her, and by now the horse was a responsive and well-trained partner.

Now he did her bidding, taking her without fuss up the steep slope at the rear of the escarpment to the plateau above the mill. Here the stream plunged out and down into the mill-race. It was a lovely spot in the strengthening moonlight. Andrea tied Boyo just below the edge of the hill with a loose knot she could slip quickly when she was ready to leave. Then she walked to the edge of the cliff overlooking the village. What she saw pleased her very much.

There were many lights on at The Stag. Dark figures ran hither and yon, shouting. The voices came up to her clearly. All through the village, windows showed yellow as candles and lamps were lighted. She would have a fine audience before long!

Stooping down, she brought out the tinder and flint and, scratching up piles of leaves and twigs, laid the straw sheaf upon the heap and ignited it. It flamed so quickly that she had to jump back to escape the fire. She gave an involuntary cry. Then she recovered her poise and stood behind the flame, lifting her arms in a way that made the draped veil look like great filmy wings. The bright blaze reflected from her chalk-white face.

To make sure the "apparition" was observed, Andrea uttered a mournful wail. The men's voices faded into silence as the people in the street caught sight of the phantom figure, flame-lit, on the cliff. Then the straw burned out and only the moonlight was left to illuminate the ghostly figure lifting its arms against the night sky.

Curiously displeased, Andrea turned and ran back to Boyo. As she bundled up her draperies to mount, she realized that her performance had been almost childishly theatrical. Surely no one would believe that the dead woman had come back to haunt the scene of her death! This was the enlightened eighteenth century, not the dark ages! Still, she had better get on with the plan, and get away from the mill before someone came to investigate. She only hoped her ruse had drawn attention to this side of the village, so she could carry out the rest of her plan safely. Somehow she didn't think that Lord Justin, even with a guilty conscience, would be too badly shaken by reports of a ghostly visitant.

Following her timetable, Andrea urged Boyo down the back of the hill and by way of a narrow lane approached the sea some distance north of the Castle. There was a narrow gully leading down to the sand somewhere here—yes, she had it—the footpath was treacherous but Boyo was sure-footed. She gave the horse his head, and he negotiated the difficult descent carefully. Then they were on the sand, almost white in the moonlight, and far above them, to the left, loomed the great Castle. It was even more imposing from this angle, the girl decided, with its mighty battlements bathed in silver light. How fine it must be, thought the girl, to be the master of this great stronghold! Her own father, little though he relished the responsibility, had yet a fierce pride in his ancestral home. Thinking of Count Vladimir, struck down in the common street so far from his own country, Andrea's resolve hardened. Fine daughter of a noble house she was, to harbor any but the fiercest feeling of anger and hatred toward the murderer!

Quickly she directed the horse to the sand at the edge of the incoming tide. There the footing was firm, the horse could move quickly. There also the rising tide would wipe out Boyo's prints. Andrea rode rapidly along the shore, a strange figure with draperies flying out behind her like mist. She turned her face up to look at the castle when she was directly below it. There were many great, lighted windows, and she saw at least two guards leaning out of embrasures to watch her. They were not shouting, but as she looked away, she noticed that one of them disappeared from his post.

Fear lurched in her breast. She must not be caught. These men were trained soldiers. They would not be easily frightened. She could expect a sally out of the Castle to challenge her within minutes. Andrea gave Boyo the office to gallop full out, and the beautiful beast obeyed her. The flying ghost-like figure shot across the sand as though on wings. When she was well beyond the Castle, Andrea pulled rein gently. Boyo, pleased with his performance, came obediently to a halt.

"You loved that, didn't you?" the girl crooned. "Well, so did I. I hope we'll be able to do it again under other circumstances. Now I want you to go back to the stables, Boyo!"

She removed the saddle and bridle and slapped the horse sharply. "Home, Boyo!"

Waiting just long enough to make sure that Boyo was trotting along the path which would eventually join the cart-track to the village, the girl hastily pulled off the green dress and veil, her riding boots, breeches, shirt and binder. Tying the dress and veil to one stirrup, she lifted the gear and the clothing and ran into the sea. The water was so cold that she almost screamed, but this was no time for feminine weakness. Dragging the heavy load after her, she swam out to deeper water. It would never have done to have one horse return saddled when the stableboys collected the strayed animals.

When she was far enough out—and thank Heaven the sea was relatively calm!—Andrea dropped the saddle and bridle thankfully. With them went the green dress and the veil. Now there was nothing to connect her with the masquerade. She had hoped, in London, that she might make several appearances as the ghost, but that was before she had encountered the vigilance of Lord Justin's men. It would be enough to come out of this one escapade safely, the girl thought, stroking towards shore. Disastrous to be caught naked on the beach, however!

Thus it was with headlong haste that she ran back up the beach to the shelter of the cliff where she had left her clothing. Shivering, she struggled into the breeches. Impossible to get them and the boots on over wet feet! She sacrificed the thick binding cloth she wore about her breasts to use it as a towel. That was better! Soon the breeches and boots were on, and the white shirt. A dab of white on one hand reminded her with a thrill of horror that she had nearly forgotten to remove the cosmetic paste on her face! The damp binder was useful for that, also, to wipe off the pigment with the small pot of cream the apothecary had supplied for that purpose. She buried the binder deep in the sand at the foot of the cliff, and brushed a heap of small rocks over the spot. Now she was ready!

She began her walk down the beach to the path she had sent Boyo to follow. She was nowhere near being out of Kyle territory. Her only hope was that Justin's people would be so occupied on the beach and around the mill that she might slip through to the inn unobserved. At the top of the path, where it came out on the cliff, Andrea peered out cautiously before taking her run across the plateau. It was well she did. From the castle came two men on horseback, pounding down toward the southern pathway to the beach. Andrea had just time to roll behind the scrub pines at the head of the path before the riders were there, slowing at the last minutes and turning their mounts into the downward trail with superb skill. Then they were gone, and the girl scuttled across the open space and into the trees without thought of dignity. A good distance to her left, Castle Kyle blazed with the light of lanterns and torches. To her right, south along the coast, there were other lights marking a mansion which belonged to a nobleman, Sir Ormand Talon. She had heard of him only one morning, when, more to divert the serving wench's too obvious personal interest than in a search for information, Andrea had enquired,

"Does Lord Justin own the whole county?"

The girl had answered with rounded eyes, "Oh, no, sir! There's another nobleman has a great house just south along the seacoast. He used to be a friend of his lordship's, but . . . they aren't so friendly of late."

"What is this nobleman's name?" Andrea was pleased that the topic was diverting the maid's attention from flirtation.

"It's Sir Ormond Talon, sir. The Talons have had the place for dunnamany years—maybe a hundred, even. 'Twas sold by his lordship's ancestor to Sir Ormand's—they were best friends. Mostly the Talons have been good friends to Kyle, but this one has always been jealous of us. We're the great house, you see," the girl ended with naive pride. Mistress Applegate called her to her duties soon after, so Andrea had been spared her childish efforts at flirtation.

Now as she stared around nervously, Andrea wondered if she should try to get to Talon House, to pretend she had wanted to see it by moonlight when Justin's guards caught her, as they were bound to. Perhaps if she humbled herself and asked for another chance—?

No! She would try to get back to the inn as she had originally planned. If they caught her, Lord Justin's guards could only humiliate her, for no harm had been done to life or property tonight. Surely even Lord Justin's men would not do more than force her to pack and be on the road back to England? Or would they? Gathering together her tattered courage, Andrea set out through the woods toward the village.

Chapter Nine

AFTER ALL HER FEARS AND QUALMS, it was almost anti-climactic to gain The Stag itself before she encountered any of Milord's men. There were lights everywhere, and the inn door yawned open upon the road, but no one was in sight. Slipping inside, Andrea went through to the kitchen and so out the back door to the stables. Enough lanterns burned to make the inside of the stable bright as daylight. Ostlers were leading horses into stalls while several men in Milord's leather were examining each horse minutely.

Andrea glanced quickly around. No one had noticed her yet, and she must make what capital she could of a strong attack. She noticed one of the patrolmen had leaned his heavy staff against the doorway, probably to leave him free to use both hands in examining the horses. Quietly she took up the cudgel and advanced into the stable. Her Boyo was being led into the lantern light. It couldn't have been better if she had planned it! The girl smiled.

"Stop, thief!" she cried in her deepest voice.

Lord Justin's men whirled to face the slight figure that challenged them. Andrea did not give them time to speak—*toujours l'audace!*—but advanced steadily, her weapon thrusting at them like a sword. To one side she noticed Applegate wringing his hands. Then he and the patrolmen spoke at once, a confused babble of threats, recriminations, and excuses.

"Call the constable!" demanded Andrea with relish.

"What is this?" demanded a cold voice from the doorway.

Andrea turned swiftly, on guard and ready to lunge. It was Milord Justin. He took his time scrutinizing her position. "Very pretty," he commented finally.

But Andrea had the bit in her teeth and was on the attack. "You are descending to horse-stealing, sir?" she asked, pointing to Boyo, out of his stall and rolling his eyes at the unaccustomed lights and bustle.

"My men were investigating—"

Andrea didn't let him finish. She wanted to keep him off balance. "You are the law here, Milord, as well as the chief landowner?"

Lord Justin controlled his temper with an effort. "Some malicious person has sought to terrorize the village with a fraudulent ghost—"

"The men of this village are afraid of *ghosts?*" she underlined the word contemptuously. "It is not so at Oxford."

Justin's eyes flashed, but he set his lips. "We do not permit the playing of dangerous pranks. Perhaps you will explain where you have spent the evening?"

"I shall be happy to," retorted Andrea sweetly, "when you have explained what your—*men* are doing with my horse."

There was a hiss of indrawn breaths at this open defiance of the master of Kyle.

"We are seeking to discover what horse it is which has been used by the prankster who sought to hoax the village tonight."

"You tracked the villain to this stable?"

"Someone turned all the horses loose. The stableboy says he saw a—ghost."

"But of course he was mistaken," supplied Andrea.

"Did you not see the fire upon the cliff above the mill?" queried Milord, suddenly affable. "While you were out about your nocturnal business? Just what was that business, Mr. Bartholomew? You were about to tell us."

"I was with a lady. Of course I cannot mention her name."

That ought to give him pause! It came straight out of the most popular novel of the day.

Milord's lips twitched. His arrogant gray glance moved up and down her person, from the neat black riding boots to the tousled golden curls. Before she could get her guard up, Milord's sinewy hand shot out and touched her head. "Your hair seems to be damp, sir. Were you perchance swimming in the millpond with—the lady in question?"

Andrea grinned. She knew she presented the figure of a spoiled and saucy youth, out womanizing at a shockingly early age. But better to

107

accept Milord's amused contempt for that than to let him get a suspicion of the truth. She lifted one slender hand to her damp curls and squeezed out some moisture, bringing it to her mouth.

"Salt," she said pertly. "My friend and I were sea-bathing."

Milord was startled into comment. "At this time of year? Did not the lady find it bitterly cold?"

"I managed to keep her reasonably warm," said Andrea outrageously.

There was a shout of laughter from the listening rustics, and even the master of Kyle grinned reluctantly. "You young scamp! You present the appearance of a prudish young angel, but your behavior is that of a hell-born babe!"

"Oh, Milord, not 'prudish,' would you say?"

Andrea found she was enjoying this encounter with Milord Justin more than any conversation she had ever taken part in. Where was the arrogant tyrant who had threatened her earlier? She smiled up into his face, with no notion of how attractive and innocent that open smile was. Milord returned it almost involuntarily, but his expression put Andrea forcibly in mind of a well-fed tiger. A faint prickle of alarm filtered into her complacency. She was playing a terribly dangerous game and she knew it, but not for nothing was she the daughter of Count Vladimir and the sister of Pola Wasylyk. All the years of careful training at the Swiss Academy could not eradicate completely the fiery

Wasylyk independence, the wilful intelligence which expressed itself as suavely trenchant wit in Count Vladi and as outrageous daring in Pola. So when Milord questioned further, "You saw nothing unusual on the beach?" Andrea slanted a wicked look at him from under her lashes.

She paused, and everyone waited for the answer. The girl permitted the silence to go on too long. Then she said in her deep, boyish voice, "Nothing *unusual*," and grinned like an urchin. "*Interesting,* but not—unusual."

Stacia would have been horrified and condemnatory. The men guffawed. Lord Justin did not seem to be amused.

"If I were your guardian, you unregenerate young rascal—" he began.

"I am fortunate that my guardian is not—prudish," said Andrea in a meditative tone.

"Do not carry your disrespect too far," warned Lord Justin. "I believe, in the interests of justice and the public weal, I must ask you to name your witness—quite between us, of course," he added gently. "No one but the two of us needs to know the lady's name." His gesture dismissed the men.

The tingle of fear became a distinct shock as Andrea realized that her inquisitor had not been fobbed off at all, but only biding his time until her wariness had abated. As the servants and the innkeeper, reluctant to miss the show, slowly left the stable, Lord Justin said softly,

"Would it be the very pretty kitchenmaid who accompanied you, boy?"

Andrea cast an agonized look toward the inn, all too conscious of the fact that Freda's partiality had been ill-disguised. Now Milord would ask her if Mr. Bartholomew had been with her, and of course the silly girl would say no! As she turned to answer Milord, she caught sight of Ben lurking just outside the stable, his face black with anger.

"Good God! Do you tell me she is Ben's sweetheart?"

Milord, watching the all too expressive countenance with satisfaction, said jovially, "I believe Ben has shown a marked interest in that direction. I'm afraid you've made an enemy."

"But you're wrong! Freda was not with me tonight, I swear!"

"Too late!" Milord advised her brightly. "Ben is out of hearing. Your gallant attempt to save a lady's name is gone for naught."

"It wasn't a gallant attempt," retorted Andrea sullenly. "I really wasn't with the girl."

"No, I was pretty sure you were not. But it is a fact that your horse was coming along the path from the ocean when my men caught him. I wonder if riding bareback is among your talents?"

"What are you implying?" challenged Andrea, who really did not want to know.

"I am telling you that the—ghost must not ride again."

Lord Justin held up a hand to silence Andrea's

protest. "I don't know how you did it, or why, for that matter. I intend to investigate carefully, and if I find a way to tie you into this ridiculous masquerade, I shall see you brought up to stand your trial. Whether tonight's episode is merely a stupid, vicious little prank, or something more sinister, I advise you to pack up and leave in the morning. Do I make myself understood?"

When Andrea did not reply, Lord Justin went out of the stable. After a few minutes Andrea heard the party from the Castle ride away. She went to comfort Boyo and see that he was settled for the night. While she was seeing to the horse's comfort, Applegate came into the stable. He appeared ill at ease.

"Will you be leaving in the morning, young sir?"

"No," answered the girl shortly. The more she thought about Lord Justin's overbearing manner, the more she longed to defy him.

"But his lordship *said*—"

"I shall leave in a couple of days. I believe that my work will be finished by then." Finished—or given up as useless, Andrea thought despairingly. It was all so different than she had imagined it would be, sitting securely in the elegant town house, with servants to do her slightest bidding, and Cousin Stacia accepting Andrea's plan with flattering confidence in its successful outcome. We have read too many romances from the lending library, Stacia and I, thought the girl. Virtue is not always rewarded, Samuel Richardson to the contrary.

Suddenly she felt very tired indeed, and it showed in the small, high-bred face.

The innkeeper was embarrassed. Whatever was Milord thinking of, to be fair hounding this stripling who hadn't a vicious bone in him, Sam Applegate was willing to swear!

"I'm sure that will suit his lordship," he said placatingly. Like his good wife, he felt a certain sympathy for the high-metalled youth, in spite of his lack of respect for the master of Kyle.

"Does everyone always do as his lordship says?" enquired Andrea bitterly. "How fortunate that is for him!"

"Now, now, young sir," soothed the innkeeper. "You've seen enough of the great world, surely, to know that it is ever thus! We must all do our best in that station to which Heaven has seen fit to call us." Then, abandoning piety for his natural voice, he added, "Or we find ourselves in a nasty pickle with the nobs, and don't you forget *that,* young Master Scholar!"

Chapter Ten

THE NEXT MORNING AT BREAKFAST, young Mr. Bartholomew was unusually quiet. William watched him for a while as they ate, and then ventured a question.

"Does your arm pain you, Bart?"

Andrea, who had managed to get herself to sleep by taking the second of Milord's painkilling powders, was understood to say that she had had a fairish night.

"I'm glad of that, for the word is out that you have been as good as told to leave by our local tyrant," William advised her. "When do you go?"

"In a day or so," muttered Andrea, presenting the very picture of a disgruntled youth.

William smiled thinly. Glancing up, Andrea caught the grimace, and wondered, as she had before, just what was keeping Mr. William himself in the vicinity. She was finding it hard to believe that this self-possessed, knowledgeable man was the idle poet he tried to represent himself as. In fact, when he was not thinking of his role, his conversation completely lacked those flights of verbiage with which he had initially greeted her. Could it be that he, too, had an ulterior purpose in being here? He seemed more the man of action than the man of letters. Could he—shocking thought—be investigating the death of Pola also? If so, at whose instigation? Chiding herself for incorrigible romanticism, the girl still found herself trying to read the purpose behind Mr. William's strong, handsome face.

William had put down his cup and was staring at her. "I have news which might interest you," he began. "It seems that an English nobleman and his wife have come to stay at the Kyle Arms. These visitors have requested an interview with the master of Kyle. He is to receive them for dinner this very evening. Their name is Castane." He watched her sharply.

Andrea's face remained unconcerned. She had never heard of the people, not did she see how their arrival could affect her plans. Apparently satisfied that she had no knowledge of the newcomers, William went on in a more relaxed manner, "It is said that they are here to bring some sort of news in connection with Milord Justin's late wife."

Andrea dropped her fork with a small clatter onto her plate.

"This intelligence bothers you, boy?"

Andrea managed a scornful smile. "Bothers me? No, I find it rather boring. I was merely a little surprised at your skill in picking up the local gossip—and at your apparent relish for it." She laughed. "Still, in a place where so little happens, these small crumbs of tittle-tattle can be exciting."

Mr. William's face was showing color at her mockery. "Did anyone ever suggest to you, halfling, that your damned impudence might earn you a broken head?" Then he tried for a recover. With a leer, he said, "My informant was Freda, that very susceptible wench who works in the kitchen. Having failed to attract you, she let me persuade her to—er—walk in the woods . . ."

His smile was openly jeering now. "You're a deal too nice in your tastes, Bart. Freda's a warm armful, and would be gentle with you." he laughed. "By God, you're blushing!"

Andrea curled her lip disdainfully, not wishing to engage in repartee of this nature lest she say something inappropriate to the character she was portraying. Finally, since the wretched man kept grinning at her, she said tartly, "I am not much in the petticoat line, sir. My sisters have given me a distaste for female artifice."

"They must be formidable indeed, to have accomplished that at your age! How many have you?"

"Five," said Andrea firmly, determined to tell a convincing lie. "All older than myself, all enjoying extreme sensibility of the nerves, and all given to ordering me about."

"Good God, boy, it's no wonder you choose to rusticate in this forsaken corner of the kingdom during your vacation from college!" William regarded the unfortunate brother with compassion. "The marvel to me is that you can encounter *any* female with common civility."

"I don't," said Andrea, recalling the kitchenmaid's advances and her laughter.

"You must be in a fair way of becoming a complete misanthrope," grinned William, but there was real emotion behind his bantering tone. "I dislike the sex myself," he admitted.

"You!" Andrea showed incredulity. "You just finished saying that that very forthcoming maid was a—a warm armful!"

"So she is. You don't have to like 'em to enjoy 'em. Just remember never to trust a woman." This was said with such vicious emphasis that Andrea decided Mr. William was not only endeavoring to instruct his young companion in the secret lore of manhood, but also expressing his real feeling about womankind. Is this really how they think of us? she mused. Is it always a secret battle, a jockeying for power, a never-relaxed distrust? Andrea felt this was very sad, if true. The novels in the lending library were not proving to be much practical help, it would seem!

Perhaps fortunately, at this moment, Applegate appeared in the doorway. He was frowning and rubbing his hands.

"Mr. Bartholomew, Ostler tells me your saddle is gone. Do you know—?"

"My saddle? But was it not racked as usual after I last used it?"

"To best of Ostler's recollection, it were, but where it can have got to, no one knows, seemingly. I would have you know 'tis first time every any such has happened at The Stag."

"Some light-fingered farmboy, perchance?" suggested William.

Applegate seemed disproportionately angry. "None of 'em 'd dare!" he snapped. "Milord is very strict, you see, and cannot be swayed from his judgment, once given."

"Right out of the Old Testament," remarked William. "A jealous god."

The innkeeper looked affronted. He pointedly addressed Andrea. "What was you wishful to do about your saddle, sir?"

"It may have fallen down behind something, in all the bustle we had when the horses were let loose," soothed Andrea. "Just supply me with another for my ride this morning. You can do that? I shall be happy to pay."

"Of course, Mr. Bartholomew, and there will be no charge."

"Thank you! Then have the local saddlery send over a selection later this afternoon. It is time I had a new saddle. I'll purchase one before I return to London."

The host seemed at once relieved and uneasy at this speech. It transpired that he feared his lordship would be angry at a theft occurring in his bailiwick; at the same time he welcomed the idea that the controversial youth was indeed preparing to quit the inn. Eventually he bowed himself out.

"You will not be embarrassed by the expense of a new saddle?" queried Mr. William.

"No, I believe I have sufficient funds for that," Andrea reassured him, rather absent-mindedly. She was thinking hard about the best use to which she could put her few final hours. She was compelled to admit that her foray into Milord's territory had resulted in nothing but humiliation for herself. Sternly she denied the vagrant memory of excitement and shared laughter, and the kindness of the gift of pain-relieving drugs for her arm. After all, he had struck her, the beast, and it was little enough that he make amends with the drugs! Rigorously she repressed the knowledge that her own amazing imprudence in accusing him of murder had brought the reprisal upon her. Pushing back from the table, she rose and sketched a boyish bow to Mr. William.

"I must thank you for your instruction concerning the sex, sir," she said in her small deep voice.

William grinned and waved her off. "It's clear to me that you were born to be hanged," he chuckled, but his eyes followed the slight boyish figure. A small frown wrinkled his forehead.

Andrea had decided upon a bold plan. She lacked the means—and, be it admitted, the nerve—to make the ghost ride again. But there might be one more place where she could discover something which would prove or disprove her suspicions of the lord of Kyle. She intended to ride to Talon House and crave an audience with its master, Sir Ormond Talon. Now what could her pretext be?

It was a glorious day, right out of summer, and Andrea straightened her shoulders and breathed deeply as she cantered along on Boyo. That intelligent beast too seemed to be enjoying the exercise, for he capered and pranced, caracoled and curveted, praticing some of the paces Andrea had taught him in order to beguile the tedium of the trip north. Andrea was laughing with delight as they came into the clearing beside a pond and came face to face with Milord Justin.

Surprise was wiped from his face by rising anger.

"*You—!* Trespassing again? Defying me again? We'll see about that!" and Milord sprang his great black stallion directly at her.

Not for nothing had Andrea been taught to ride by a Cossack officer. Not for nothing had she schooled and talked to Boyo on the trip to Kyle Village and on all their rides since. With a quick prod of knee and toe, she whirled the horse in his own length and sent him galloping off back along the path they had just quitted. Behind her the stallion's hooves beat an angry tattoo at the earth, but were they coming nearer? No; by all that was wonderful, she was drawing ahead! Andrea laughed.

Whether she had misjudged the speed of Milord's advance, or whether the sound of her mocking laughter had angered him to increased effort, Andrea was not to know. The first warning she had was a flash, from the side of her eye, of a great ebon head, eyes aglare, coming

119

up at her left shoulder. Within seconds Milord's horse was level with Boyo and was crowding him ruthlessly off the path. Andrea shouted encouragement to her horse, and gave him his head, but to no avail. Milord thrust ahead and began to rein in his stallion across the path.

Andrea couldn't believe her luck. With another low-voiced command and a touch of her knee, she caused Boyo to whirl, cat-like, and race back the way they had come. The audacity of this move, and Boyo's quick comprehension and performance, so excited and pleased her that Andrea gave a shout of triumph. It was her undoing. Behind her the great stallion trumpeted and thundered after the fleeing duo. Thoroughly aroused, Lord Justin was not to be bested. Within seconds his black had come up again beside Boyo's shoulder and was jostling the smaller horse off the path.

Andrea took one look at the furious anger on Milord's face and gave Boyo the office to break stride. She could not let her gallant friend be forced into the underbrush and perhaps injured.

So, under guard, Boyo and his rider came again into the small clearing by the pond. Milord's stallion loomed over them, eyes rolling, and his master, features rigidly controlled, stared at Andrea.

Facing that ice-gray scrutiny, the girl quailed.

"I was on my way to visit Sir Ormond," she offered in a small voice.

"If that is true, you had lost your way. This road leads to Kyle Castle." Could anything be colder than his voice? Somehow it was worse than red rage. "I cannot believe you did not know it," Milord continued.

Unbidden, the memory of Applegate's words rose into Andrea's mind. "Milord is very strict, and cannot be swayed from his judgment, once given."

She forced herself to meet the big man's gaze bravely. "On my word, Lord Justin, I intended no trespass this time. I truly believed I was on the road to Talon House." Why, Mr. William himself had pointed it out to her as she left the inn!

There was a silence broken only by the heavy breathing of the horses as Milord considered her statement. Still holding her gaze steadfast, Andrea continued. "I admit to imprudence in my speech the last time I addressed your lordship, and for that I ask your pardon. I do not know quite how it is, but when I come to talking to you—" her expressive little face echoed the bewilderment expressed by her uplifted, open palms. Then a flush rose in her cheeks as she heard herself make these apologetic, *truckling* remarks. What was the matter with her? Generations of Wasylyks would whirl in their honorable graves at such a crawling speech from their unworthy descendant! She straightened her shoulders and lifted her chin. "That is all I have to say."

"Is it? I suppose I should be thankful for small mercies," replied Milord, staring hard at the flushed, handsome face. The ice-hardness seemed to be melting out of his countenance, and a reluctant twitch at one corner of his strong, beautifully-cut mouth indicated that his anger was abating. He looked from Andrea to her mount. "That was rather good riding," he said at last.

Andrea smiled shyly. "Thank you."

Milord grinned. "We both know it was superb," he admitted. "With a stronger horse, you'd have given me the slip. Where—how—did you learn to ride like that, boy?"

Andrea's rush of pleasure at his praise was completely voided by the next remark. "I might be willing to hire you as my groom. Such expertise should not be wasted."

"I am not for hire," said Andrea, very stiff and haughty.

"Here's a fine heat!" Milord was regaining his good temper rapidly. "Perhaps I shall arrest you for trespass, and impose a sentence of sixty days hard labor—in my stables." His smile challenged her.

"I am leaving Kyle Village tomorrow," protested Andrea, "and I gave you my word I did not intend to trespass today!"

"You think, then, that I should accept the word of a vagrant youth who refuses to present his credentials?"

Andrea felt her spirits sink. Was she to go through all that again? And what could she say? It was impossible to tell the truth, and she hadn't any documents to prove her assumed name and sex. Unconsciously her glance met Milord's with appeal.

He watched her for a moment, then said softly, "Get off your horse."

"M-m-ilord?"

"Off!"

Andrea slipped neatly down and stood to Boyo's head.

"A well-trained animal and a remarkable rider. It seems a pity not to learn more about you, Master Enigma. But if you give your word you are leaving tomorrow—?"

"Oh, yes, Lord Justin!" said Andrea so devoutly that a reluctant smile came to the big man's lips.

"I think there should be some punishment for the trouble you have caused me, and certainly for your impudence, do not you?"

"Punishment?" faltered Andrea, wide-eyed.

"We are quite alone and unobserved here. Perhaps the rules of chivalry might be set in abeyance for once—since neither one of us happens to be wearing his sword. As for fisticuffs, I have a trifle the advantage of you in weight and reach—" He was openly grinning at her now, as he slid from his great stallion and walked over to stand beside her. "Shall we let our good beasts do token battle for us?"

Horrified at the idea, Andrea stared from Boyo to the huge monster Lord Justin rode. "That would be terribly unfair! I cannot think your lordship is serious! Besides, I am sure Boyo doesn't know how to fight."

"He could learn, if attacked," advised Milord dryly. "What then do you suggest? Personal battle between us two?"

"You are pleased to jest, Milord," said Andrea sternly.

Lord Justin broke into a shout of laughter. "I am indeed, my bantling. I also cannot quite understand the effect you have upon me, you impudent young jackanapes, but I find it difficult to stay angry with you. And yet you must not be allowed to leave my demesne without a lesson of some sort—" He cast his glance around. "A caning, do you think? There are plenty of stout branches to hand . . ."

Andrea made a quick move to remount. A hard hand caught her firmly by the upper arm. "I think not. I believe I have already bruised your person sufficiently. So what else, educational and yet not too painful in its effects?"

Outraged at this teasing, Andrea turned her head to glare at her tormentor. At that moment he bent and swung her into his arms, strode rapidly toward the pond, and tossed her in.

She landed with a mighty splash. Muddy water rushed into her mouth, opened to shout. Coughing and spluttering, she struggled to her feet. The water was waist deep. Above her choking she heard his mocking laughter. "Another swim for you, bantling! Such a nice day for it, too!"

As she began to wade ashore, her foot slipped on the slimy mud bottom of the pond and she fell in again. Clenching her fists in rage, she once again got to her feet and waded more carefully out of the water.

Lord Justin was mounted by this time. He was watching her with considerable amusement. "At least there was no audience to your downfall this time," he mocked.

After one scathing glance, rather hindered by the strand of soggy weeds over her face, the girl turned and made for her own horse.

"Just be sure you are out of Kyle Village by tomorrow night, Bartholomew, or you will find yourself answering questions. This is my last warning." He turned and rode off down the forest path.

Hideously uncomfortable, muttering under her breath, and trying not to cry, Andrea rode slowly after him.

Chapter Eleven

POLA'S ghost rode again that night.

The first that Andrea knew of the matter was when she was roused from a very uneasy slumber by shouts and cries from the taproom below her. She had come back to the stables after her encounter with Lord Justin in a grim temper, drenched and shivering, her clothing offensive to her nostrils from the pond muck, and to her delicate skin from the damp chafing. She had had to endure crude jests from the stableboy, and to cap it all, the ostler told her she'd have to pay for any damage done to the borrowed saddle because of the soaking it had received on the ride home. Leaving them guffawing over their own wit, she stalked into the kitchen, ordered a hot bath at once, and stamped up to her room. The wait for the hot water—for she could not divest herself of her wet garments until the maid had come and gone—did nothing to improve her temper. And when Freda, bringing the second two cans of water, offered to wash Mr. Bartholomew's back for him, it was the last straw. Mr. Bartholomew dismissed the saucy piece with an oath Andrea didn't realize she knew. Then, locking the door, she stripped off the noisome garments—ruined, she decided glumly—and sank into the blessed warmth in the huge old tub. Having to get out again to fetch her soap, which in her haste she had forgotten, did nothing to restore the tone of her mind.

The hot water soothed and calmed her, and her thoughts drifted to pleasanter matters. With a sense of shock she discovered that she was thinking of Dominic Justin, the way his mouth quirked at the corners when he was trying to repress a smile, the ice-cold gray of his eyes which could amazingly become warm with laughter, the feel of his strong body as his big arms closed around her and held her secure . . . even if he was in the act of tossing her into the pond at the time!

Suddenly she sat up in the tub, grasped for the washcloth and set vigorously to scrubbing away such coy, missish maunderings. What, was she some schoolroom chit with her sighs and vaporings over the first good-looking man who came into her ken? Then Andrea gave a reluctant chuckle. She was honest and direct, two qualities she must have inherited from her mother and the sturdy middle-class grandfather. She forced herself to accept the unpalatable facts that, *primus:* she *was* little more than a schoolroom miss; *secundus:* that she had not at all the same feelings for the dark and dashing Mr. William, undeniably as good-looking as Milord; and, *tertius:* that she had been convinced for several days that Dominic Justin had not murdered her sister. The blow which had felled Andrea had been given in justifiable anger to an impudent youth, not to a girl; and sending the soothing medicine was an act of compassion. Even the throwing into the pond of a persistently annoying boy—for she knew she was that and no more to Milord—was not the act of a vicious murderer.

Conclusio: (I am being very logical, Andrea congratulated herself) Lord Justin had not killed Pola; therefore she had indeed died by accident, just as her wilful mother had done, or—her mind continued relentlessly—Pola had been murdered by someone else! Unbidden, the name of Sir Ormond Talon flashed into her mind. For the first time, Andrea began to realize that she was meddling in matters of desperate intrigue. This was no romantic tale to be resolved with a neat confession or simple ingenuity. This was mystery and dark passion and hatred leading to ruthless murder. She would go back to London at once, the very next day, for it was too late to set out today, and leave the solving of crimes to those who were trained and competent to handle such business.

As for Lord Justin—she forced herself to admit that she could never mean anything to that arrogant man, for had he not married her sister? Was there not a law against a man marrying his sister-in-law? So she would return to her own milieu, try to grow up into a sensible woman, and eventually marry some quite worthy young man who would have strong arms and a hard warm chest and who would look exactly like Lord Justin!

When she had come to this logical conclusion, Andrea dried herself hastily, flung herself into bed, and cried herself to sleep.

A few hours later, she became aware, with some alarm, of the commotion in the inn. Men shouted, doors banged, there was even a shot fired in the road almost beneath her window. With shaking fingers she lit the candles and struggled to find some clothing that wasn't soaked with slimy mud. Fresh underclothing and a shirt were available, woolen stockings ready to hand, but her one good suit, put on for calling at Talon House, was ruined. She fumbled out her riding breeches, the last of those made by her father's order, now just a little too tight. Putting them on, she thrust her shirt into the waist band and sat down to pull on her old riding boots. She stood up, stamping the boots on. Now, what to do for a coat? There was only her father's driving coat, but it was both warm and concealing—excellent qualities in this situation. Running the brush casually through her curls, Andrea opened the door and descended to the front hallway.

Freda was busy lighting all the lamps. Andrea noted sourly that the girl had either been been dressed when the trouble began or had taken time to titivate herself, for her hair was in its usual artful disarray over her smooth brown shoulders, and her dress, without the modest fichu Mistress Applegate normally insisted upon, was an invitation to any masculine eyes in the neighborhood.

"Oh, lawks, Mr. Bartholomew, 'tis the ghost again!" she squawked. Andrea was pleased to note that her voice was not at all enticing.

"You have seen a ghost?"

Freda shook her head. " 'Twas Joe saw it, out in stable."

"Again?" mocked Andrea. Joe was the unfortunate stableboy who had beheld her on that other, haunted night, and promptly fainted.

But Freda was protesting. "Jem Ostler saw it too. All draped in white an' creepin' near the earth it was, Jem says. Fair give 'im a turn!"

Andrea stopped smiling. This was no drunken recapitulation of her earlier phantom. The picture conjured up by Freda's words was a singularly unpleasant one. Repressing a shudder, Andrea went out of the inn to join a small group of villagers who were standing in the road. Some of them held torches, and the flickering light on tense faces gave the scene a macabre quality.

"So there you are, Mr. Bartholomew," said a voice which Andrea identified as belonging to her host. "We are wondering if you were going to sleep through it all."

"How could anyone?" snapped Andrea crossly. "Such a hubbub over a stableboy's nightmare!"

"Nightmare it were not, young master,"

130

objected Applegate, and half a dozen voices bore him out. "Will Stout, he's with the local militia, just back from the army is Will, and brought his blunderbuss wi' him—he fired off at the ghost smart enough and sent it packin' toward the Castle!"

"Did he do it any harm?" asked Andrea, convinced that there was a human agency behind this latest appearance of the ghost.

There was a scandalized tut-tutting from the crowd.

"Now how could a blunderbush harm a unquiet spirit?" asked one villager sternly.

"The English have no respect for tradition," said a voice which Andrea thought she recognized as that of the local schoolmaster, Dominie Burkett, with whom she had avoided a conversation about Oxford in the taproom of Kyle Arms. He had not forgiven her for her imagined slight.

A third voice said sharply, "It's them colleges addlin' the minds of young folk!" Whereat the cultured voice of Dominie Burkett retorted, "Hold your tongue, Tamson!" It was clear that while he might disapprove of one individual student, he was in no way prepared to let anyone defame education.

"Sorry, Dominie," came the rather unconvincing apology.

Andrea fought a sense of unreality. "Then why, if it could do no harm, did Will South fire his blunderbush—*buss?*" she challenged. What am I doing getting into an argument over unquiet spirits, she wondered, with reluctant amusement, and the thought crossed her mind of the pleasure Lord Justin would take in this situation.

There was a cry from someone in the group, and everyone's attention was diverted toward two mounted figures advancing down the road toward the inn. Upon closer inspection, these were seen to be Jem the ostler and Will Stout, the young farmer militiaman who was generally known to be soft on Freda. This fact probably explained why he had been able to get to his horse so quickly when the alarm first broke out in the stable. The two were at once besieged with questions as to the outcome of the chase. The intelligence which they were able to import was startling enough to silence the group momentarily.

" 'Twas Mr. William playin' ghost," said Jem, proud to be the bearer of such a dramatic piece of news. "We ran 'im along Castle road ... hollerin' fit to wake dead! 'E was gettin' away from us—powerfu' little 'orse 'e 'ad, when who should come ridin' 'ell-for-leather down road but 'is lordship an' two of the guards. 'Twas Ben an' Matt, an' all three o' them spoilin' for a fight."

"They got it!" added the young farmer with relish. "William fought like a devil—yellin' at 'em in a foreign tongue, an' flashin' a nasty long blade. Got Lord Justin wi' it."

Andrea felt a wave of faintness sweep over her. "Lord Justin ... is dead?" she whispered.

But other stronger voices were clamoring for an answer, and to her inexpressible relief, Jem replied, "No. Just a monstrous deep cut on left arm. Matt bound it wi' 'is lordship's own neckerchief."

The young farmer took up the tale with relish. "When 'is lordship disarmed William, Matt an' Ben wrestled 'im down an' bound 'im to a tree at Milord's command. Then Matt tended to 'is lordship's arm, after which we was told to go 'ome and bid you all disperse to your beds." He grinned. "Up to anything, is Milord! There 'e was, wi' the blood soakin' 'is arm, sendin' us off cool as a cowcumber!"

There was a general murmur of discontent, in which Andrea found herself joining. "You mean to say you don't know what happened after that?" she asked angrily. "I for one shall not go to bed until the whole is resolved."

Although there was agreement with her sentiments, which were thought to be very sensible, Dominie Burkett said firmly. "His lordship will handle it, and we shall hear tomorrow why William tried to play the ghost, and what punishment Lord Justin visited upon him. Now let us go to our homes, all of us, for there is nothing more we can do tonight."

Some wit in the crowd suggested that Host Applegate might open up the taproom again and serve everyone a soothing potion. This was received with encouraging shouts and laughter from the group, but no compliance at all from the innkeeper. He herded his servants back into the inn and shut the great front door smartly. The villagers began to walk away in twos and threes, busily discussing the exciting events of the evening.

Andrea had faded into the shadows by the inn, and was unnoticed. After a few minutes, having given Applegate time to put out the lamps and send his servants to their beds, she crept back to the stable. Here one solitary lantern still burned, but the stableboy was nowhere to be seen. Andrea crept inside and went to Boyo's stall.

It was empty. She looked further, and saw William's bay still in its proper place. So, William had taken her horse for his midnight impersonation! Resentment rose in the girl's breast. What a scurvy trick to play! If the horse had been recognized and the culprit not caught, she would have been the prime suspect. She could not in truth dismiss the idea that William would be willing to serve her such an ill turn, yet what could have been his motive for making the ride in the first place? Why should he want the ghost of Milord's dead wife to ride through the village?

It seemed very important indeed that she discover what really lay behind this strange behavior. Without considering too clearly the possible effects of her action, Andrea deftly saddled William's bay and rode quietly out of the inn-yard. Keeping to the grassy verge of the road, where the sound of the horse's hooves was dulled, the girl made her way toward the Castle road. Once within the wood, she quickened pace and moved quietly up toward the scene of the night's bizarre action.

She did not see the torches she expected, nor hear any sound. The first warning she had was when the bay skittered nervously, whinnied, and was answered by a muffled groan. Her eyes, by now accustomed to the darkness, picked out a lighter patch near the foot of a tree. Quickly she dismounted and walked toward the tree. Mr. William was crumpled on the ground, cut ends of rope testifying to the fact that he had been held prisoner for a time. His coat and shirt, along with a torn sheet, had been ripped from him, probably by the agency of his own knife, which was disdainfully stuck through the garments, pinning them to the earth. William was leaning face downward against the tree. His back was a mass of dark stripes.

Andrea tried to lift his shoulder. With a snarl of bared teeth he flung up his head, then blinked incredulously.

"Bart! What are you doing here? I thought it was that devil come back!"

"Everyone is gone, Mr. William. Let me help you to return to the inn. You are in need of medical attention."

"Forget that! 'Tis my pride that's wounded, more than my back! I'll have revenge on that devil if I die doing it," muttered William, audibly grinding his teeth.

Shocked by his venom, Andrea yet remembered her own anger and humiliation over much less than William had suffered. A proud man could be driven to madness by such treatment. She began to try to get William to his feet and onto the back of his horse, hoping that the now nervous animal would accept its own master more readily than a stranger. She scanned the undergrowth and the road, but saw no sign of Boyo. She would have to get William on his own horse and lead them back to the inn. It would be a hard task, but not an impossible one.

Half an hour later, she thankfully brought the bay into the stable behind The Stag. The lantern had burned low, but still furnished enough light for Andrea to assist William to dismount. It was an ungraceful proceeding, but she got him to his feet and led him, shoulder under his armpit, into the inn by the kitchen door. Mounting the stairs was easier than she had feared. Her patient seemed to be recruiting his strength, and helped himself by clinging to the stairrail. They crept, soft-footed, down the corridor. William indicated his own door. Andrea got it open and helped him through and toward his bed, which showed clearly in the light coming through the uncurtained window. When the man was resting prone on his bed, Andrea closed the door quietly and lighted a candle. With it in hand, she came to the bed and looked down on William's back.

The blood from the whipping had dried; it was not as savage as Andrea had feared, although it was severe enough, she was sure, to cause much pain. She got a clean towel and dipped it in the pitcher on the washstand, then moved to wipe the blood gently from the cuts.

William roused himself. "Let be, boy. I'm well enough. A drink is what I need. Get one from the dresser top."

There was a bottle of fine French brandy on the dresser, and Andrea poured a glassful which she gave him. He tossed it down in one grateful gulp and wordlessly demanded more. Andrea filled the glass again. Perhaps the liquor would prove a painkiller. A night's sleep would enable Mr. William to face the problems which would surely confront him tomorrow. He sipped the second glass more slowly. His dark eyes glittered in the light of the candle.

"How came you to find me?" he muttered.

"I heard of the ghost . . . and the attack upon you, and went out to find you."

"Obliged," said William formally, but his mind was elsewhere. "They stripped me—even my breeches, damn them! They were looking for a woman!" He drained the glass and held it out again.

Andrea made no move to take the glass. "A *woman*? But that is . . . insane!"

"No. There is a sister of Lord Justin's wife who is missing. Those Castanes from London called to inform Justin. The girl was supposed to have gone back to her school in Switzerland, but when a friend of the family went there to offer condolences, the headmistress said she had never returned from London. Somewhere there is another red-haired, green-eyed bitch . . . loose in the world . . . damn her . . ." His voice dulled and ceased and the glass fell from his fist to the bed.

Andrea replaced it on the dresser, put out the candle, and closed the door behind her. As she crept back to her own room, the shock of what she had just heard had her brain reeling. Of course everyone in the village would have known the color of hair and eyes of Lord Justin's wife, and Mr. William had demonstrated his ability to glean information. Yet the rancor, even hatred he revealed—! Could he be someone who had *known* Pola, who perhaps had followed her to this village, and was even now seeking to avenge her death? Vengeance upon Lord Dominic Justin?

Well, why should she care for that? Painfully the girl faced the truth—that she had fallen in love with her sister's husband, and that she feared he would be injured by William. Yet it was no business of hers. She had no right to defend Lord Justin. There could be nothing between the widowed lord and his dead wife's sister. He did not even like her! While she— Andrea closed her eyes against the painful discovery of her own vulnerability. She tried to decide how to escape the net which seemed to be tightening around her. At length she laid out a fresh shirt for the morning, packed her trunk and portmanteau, locked them, and got into bed. Her course was clear to her. She must leave by first light. To remain would accomplish nothing. More, it could expose her to terrible dangers.

Chapter Twelve

ANDREA SLEPT LIGHTLY and was awake and dressed at dawn. Had it not been that she owed the innkeeper for a week's board and lodging, she might have slipped away before any of the servants were awake. She toyed with the idea of leaving an adequate sum on the dresser in her bedroom and then vanishing without a formal goodbye. However this was not to be considered seriously, for she had no wish to draw attention further upon herself by odd behavior. So, carrying her portmanteau and leaving the trunk to be sent after her, she came out of her room into the upper hallway.

As she was going past Mr. William's door she heard a groan. She hesitated, and was lost. Opening the door a trifle, she called softly, "May I do something to help?"

"Come in!" It was a desperate cry.

Misliking the weakness and pain revealed in the voice, Andrea came into the room. In the revealing morning sunlight, William presented a grim picture, stretched out on his back on the bed. His cuts had bled during the night of restless turning and tossing, and the sheet was stained. His face was haggard, his beard unshaven, and his black hair a tangle. Andrea was shocked by his appearance.

"Let me send a doctor to you! I am sure you have a fever."

"No, no, I'm well enough," muttered William, his eyes on her face.

"Your back needs attention, Mr. William. You have been cruelly used. At least I'll have the maid bring up hot tea for you."

"Don't wait for that. You must get away at once," whispered William fiercely. The girl thought his eyes had a mad light in them. "Justin has lost his self-control. He's going to strip and lash every stranger in the village. Take my horse and go at once! Head for London. Once you're safe away from here, you can take your time. I'll catch up with you on the road and get my horse back in a few days."

"Why should I take your—?" Oh!" she remembered that her own Boyo had not been in the stable. Mr. William had taken him for his ghost appearance, but the horse had not been at the scene of the whipping. Andrea frowned. Why had William taken Boyo in the first place? If it was to throw suspicion on young Bartholomew, dared she accept his advice now? There was much more to this situation than she had guessed. She began to doubt her ability to come through it without error.

William had been watching her with fevered eyes. "You will do as I say? Take my horse and make run for it? You are in very great danger, I swear before God! You do not know the evil . . .

the evil . . ." he choked and gasped, stretching out one hand piteously toward her.

Andrea came to the bed with some thought of bathing his face and straightening his bedding to make him more comfortable. He reached out and caught her wrist in sinewy fingers. His hand was hard and burning hot. He pulled her over the bed until she was nearly on top of his body. "You must get away!"

Then in one quick movement, he clipped her body close to his and ran his other hand hard across her breasts. His eyes were glaring and his lips drawn back in a snarl.

Andrea jerked herself away from him with difficulty, stumbling back a few steps. He raised himself on one elbow, trying to get off the bed after her. The girl whirled and raced from the room, not stopping to pick up her portmanteau from the hall as she ran down the front stairway. The front door was wide open, and conferring quietly with Applegate was Lord Justin!

His glanced of polite enquiry changed to guarded concern as he noted her shocked face. He came forward and met her at the foot of the stairs. "Ah, Mr. Bartholomew! Well met! I am glad to have caught you before you left."

This had an ominous sound, in spite of the imperturbability of his expression. He was such a handsome big man, point-device in his riding dress even so early in the morning, looming above her against the bright sunlight from the door, so that she could see only his big shoulders and fine head outlined in gold. If only she did not feel this treacherous weakness whenever she was in his presence! The weakness which made her force a saucy manner she did not really wish to exhibit! Andrea made her voice consciously deep and firm.

"I am leaving, sir, immediately after breakfast, as I have already informed Applegate."

"So he tells me. But I have brought that which will make your journey easier." To the question implied by her rather haughtily raised eyebrows, he pointed to the hitching post in front of the door, standing aside so that she could see Boyo tied there, well-groomed and obviously much at his ease.

Mortified, Andrea stammered her thanks. What a fool she must appear, planning to ride off without a horse! Did this man always have to get the better of her? Then it occurred to her that she was not expected to have known anything about William taking her horse for his ride, or that Boyo had not been returned last night. She made a recover.

"You have ordered him brought round for me? This is to speed the parting guest indeed!" and she essayed a smile.

"My servants—found your horse in my woods last night. It was only courtesy to return him to you this morning."

"Again, my thanks, Milord," said Andrea. "Now if you will excuse me—a cup of coffee before I begin my journey . . ." and she made to go past him into the dining room.

Perhaps it was the aftermath of the peculiar

attack which Mr. William had made upon her person; perhaps the relief of learning that Milord had returned Boyo; perhaps even the powerful male presence of Dominic Justin—for whatever reason, Andrea now experienced a wave of giddiness as she turned quickly. She was forced to catch at the doorjamb with one hand. In an instant, moving like lightning, Lord Justin was at her side and had a hand on her shoulder.

"What is it? Are you ill? I thought as you came downstairs that there was something wrong."

Toujours l'audace! She must brazen it out for just an hour more—long enough to get out of this village and safe on the road to London! "I have just had a very strange and ugly experience with Mr. William," she said in a low voice. Better to tell as much of the truth as possible to Milord from this moment—her awkward lies had a way of being exposed before his gray searching eyes. She managed to slide her shoulder out from under Milord's grip and preceded him into the dining parlor. "I had not intended to speak of it to anyone, but you, Milord, are a man of the world, so perhaps . . ."

Lord Justin nodded gravely, but again at the corners of his lips small muscles tugged in the repressed smile Andrea found so devastating. "As one man of the world to another," he said solemnly, "and also considering that I horse-whipped the rogue last night for trying to cast suspicion on you, my dear sir, I think you may count me a sympathetic listener."

"Oh, was it you who was responsible for his condition?" Andrea asked artlessly. "He seems in great pain, possibly feverish."

"He deserves it—and more," answered Milord grimly; and then, putting her firmly in her place, "But these are matters in which you can have little interest. Pray honor me with your confidence. You spoke of an ugly experience?"

Andrea moved toward the dining table and moistened her dry throat with a sip from one of the cups of coffee a nervous Freda had just poured. As soon as the girl had scuttled from the room, Andrea began, "As I was coming downstairs a few minutes ago, I heard a groan from one of the bedrooms. I pushed open the door to offer help, and was greeted by a gory sight. Mr. William was lying on the bed, obviously injured and in a fever. I advanced to his bedside to ask what I could do to help . . . when Mr. William touched my body . . . made a gesture which I could not tolerate—from another man."

The effort it took to raise her eyes from the coffee cup to Milord's face was the greatest she had ever made. She could not control the fiery color in her face, but she held her voice as steady as she could. "I had not known one man could make such a gesture to another. Oh, at school there was some talk of such behavior, but I am afraid I disregarded it." She looked away, finally. "What you have said is true,

Milord. I am not yet man enough to be away from my home. I must return at once."

Lord Justin watched the proud, embarrassed young face thoughtfully. "While I cannot be sure just what—er—gesture Mr. William sought to make upon your person," he said slowly, "I feel it only fair to the rogue to inform you that his action was more likely dictated by a desire for information than for—anything else."

"Information?" Andrea's squeak of fear might have been a youth's falsetto voice-break.

Milord nodded. "There is a rumor that a certain young lady is missing and may have come to this part of the world. I believe his action was an attempt to discover if you—" he paused deliberately, eyebrows elevated.

"I thought he was *feverish!*" exclaimed Andrea, her very real awareness of how close he was to the truth appearing as a natural embarrassment. "He is obviously out of his senses. A doctor should be sent for at once." She put down her empty cup. "I shall request Applegate to do it."

Milord made no move, but stood looking down at her soberly. It could only be by chance, Andrea hoped, that he had placed himself between her and the door.

"You have had rather a thin time of it, Scholar, on your prized first flight from the nest. Yet I think it wise of you to return home now. You have inadvertently embroiled yourself in dangerous matters. And listened to too much gossip, I fear! In future, you might consider the advisability of securing all the facts before making judgments."

"I asked your pardon for that, Milord," said Andrea stiffly. "I know now that you could never have murdered Pola or the count—"

His face had changed in a flash. With a single stride he was upon her, and had her shoulder in a stone-crushing grip.

"Whence had you that name, boy—and how dare you use it?"

"Mr. William used it," Andrea lied instinctively. "He told me the tale—"

Flinging her from him so she lost her balance, Lord Justin strode to the door and hailed the innkeeper. "Inform my servants that I wish them here at once."

Picking herself up from the floor where his anger had thrust her, Andrea went quietly to sit at the table. What a fool she was to have allowed her over-confidence in her acting ability to betray her into such a disastrous mistake! Mentioning Pola by name—and the count! At best, Lord Justin would believe her to be an insufferable gossip. At worst—? She poured herself another cup of coffee, and made a pretense of eating a slice of the bread Freda had set out. That was another thing. What was wrong with the maid? Lacking completely her normal bold, saucy manner, the girl had gotten out of the room as quickly as possible. A good suggestion for me to follow, Andrea decided fearfully. As soon as Milord moved out into the hall to speak to his servants, she would escape—through the

147

window, if necessary. What mattered trunk or portmanteau? Escape was the objective.

But Milord failed to oblige. He stood just in the doorway, filling it with his inordinate height and broad shoulders. Shortly Andrea heard the voice of Alan, Milord's factor.

"You sent for me, Milord?"

"Take another man and get William. He's abed, upstairs. Applegate will show you the room. He's to be brought to the Castle at once, and with him, everything that belongs to him—everything! He fooled us very neatly last night. He knows much more of the business than he admitted."

"Aye, your lordship." There was the heavy tramp of boots up the stairs, and the light nervous voice of Applegate.

Lord Justin came back into the dining room. "I am glad you did not try to run away," he said in a silky voice.

"There was no reason why I should." Andrea was beginning to feel out of charity with this arrogant, cold-eyed man, and to wonder why she had ever thought him attractive. "When I have finished my breakfast, I shall mount my horse and wipe the dust of this unattractive village from my feet. You are still in the middle ages here, Milord. I shall be glad to return to civilization."

Gone from Lord Justin's face was even the faintest hint of compassion or amusement. "Fine rhetoric, youngling. But may I remind you that you are still in this unattractive village, and so under my jurisdiction. Yes, you were correct. We are medieval here. I am master of Kyle, and my writ runs from the sea to the hills of Kyle at county's end." His lips moved in the coldest smile Andrea had ever seen. "I warn you, boy, I have come to the end of my patience. My power is absolute. You would be well-advised to leave quickly and quietly, before you find yourself haled up to the Castle to answer for your behavior."

Cheered by the prospect of immediate escape, Andrea became over-valiant. "But, Milord, what have I to say to any of this?"

Lord Justin sighed in exasperation. "Am I never to be rid of you, you nuisance? The only thing you can tell me is why you are wearing that ridiculous coat. It is much too large and obviously not your own. If it is William's, I shall have to ask you to leave it here."

The golden head went high, and a husky young voice spoke proudly. "The clothes I wear are clean and paid for. If they are not quite suitable, that may be forgiven in a student who has not the wealth of the master of Kyle. When you threw me in the pond, Milord, you ruined my one good suit. The coat I am wearing was my father's."

Lord Justin looked at Andrea with irritation. "Then I suppose I must offer you recompense. Come up to the Castle with your—report, or whatever it was, and I'll read it after dinner. Perhaps I could subsidize your research. I know enough not to offer money to such a young hot-head as you."

"Do you really think I would accept anything from you, Milord?" The tone of voice was an insult. Andrea was so far into her role as poor young scholar that she was quite carried away by the emotions suitable to the performance.

Lord Justin's expression hardened. "You young idiot! I've taken more impudence from you than from any man I've ever known! If you are not out of Kyle Village in ten minutes, I'll have you dragged up to the Castle along with your friend William."

Under his fiery eye, the girl scuttled thankfully out into the hall. What had possessed her to defy this tyrant? Would she *never* learn to control her childish behavior? She settled her bill with a subdued Applegate, strapped her portmanteau onto the back of Boyo's saddle, gave directions for the delivery of her trunk by the stagecoach when next it passed through Kyle Village. She was informed how to pick it up at the staging office, and, after leaving vails for the servants who had waited upon her, she made her escape into the bright sunshine at the front of the Stag with an overwhelming feeling of relief. She had not encountered Milord, for which she was devoutly thankful. She cantered rapidly down the road, out of the village, and turned southward toward London as soon as she met the highroad. Only after a good half hour of steady riding did Andrea feel safe enough to let Boyo find an easier pace. She wanted very much to look back to see if Kyle Castle was in view, but pride or something else she didn't define prevented her. He had as good as thrown her out of his territory and his life. Very well! She would put Lord Dominic Justin of Kyle, with his arrogance and his anger and his cruelty, out of her mind. Forever.

She spent the rest of the long day's ride thinking of him.

Chapter Thirteen

ANDREA DID NOT DISCOVER a suitable inn until dusk. She was beginning to get a little nervous, for she had no desire to spend a night in the open, and the few hostelries she passed were little more than taverns. Then, set back from the road behind a neat apron of grass, she saw a small, white-painted building whose swinging sign proclaimed it to be The White Charger. It was neat and most attractive, and from its open door wafted out the mouth-watering fragrance of roasting beef and onions. Andrea foolishly assumed that her troubles were over, and dismounted with a weary sigh.

As she was hitching Boyo to the post beside the door, the innkeeper came bustling out.

"I should like a room for the night, a hot bath, and then a double portion of that delectable roast beef I smell," began the girl, smiling. "Your stableboy can look after my horse, can he not?"

Mine Host's eyes ran over her ill-fitting coat, paused with brief appreciation on the good lines of Boyo, and then finished with a lightning scrutiny of her gear—or the lack of it.

"You have lost your luggage, young sir?"

"It is following me to London on the stage," said Andrea haughtily. "I travel light."

"You do indeed," agreed the innkeeper. "English, I suspect?"

"Oh, no," Andrea began thoughtlessly. Her only excuse was that she was tired, exhausted even, by the mental and physical strains of the day's ride.

Mine Host lapsed into broad lowland Scots. "Ye'll no be tellin' me ye're a Scot, will ye?"

"Oh, no! I am—I am French," the girl invented hastily. Never let it be imagined that another Pole was wandering around within a day's ride of Kyle Castle! *"C'est vrai,"* she continued with more aplomb. *"Je suis français, monsieur."*

Her accent, could Mine Host have appreciated it, was pure and elegant Parisian, but the apprehensive look on her face was more than enough for one who considered himself the shrewdest innkeeper on the highroad.

"We are none too fond of foreign folk in these parts," he said discouragingly.

Andrea flushed angrily and brought out her purse. The one thing Stacia had insisted upon, besides her restriction on entering taverns, was that Andrea carry enough money to handle any eventuality. Proudly she shook out a heaping handful of golden guineas and proferred them to her reluctant host.

"Take what you need for dinner and lodging," she ordered crisply.

"And where might a fledgling like you have gotten such a braw heap of guineas?" queried the innkeeper with even greater suspicion. "Be off wi' ye, ye young thief! I've no wish to find maself haled up before Magistrate for harborin' a criminal!"

Andrea gasped. "How dare you—?" she began, then turned to remount Boyo. The innkeeper shouted something incoherent behind her, but it did not seem that he would take steps against the supposed thief.

At that moment, like something in a nightmare, three men came riding hell-for-leather down the highroad. The big man who led them almost overshot the inn, but pulled his black stallion around so hard that its forelegs beat at the air. And then Lord Justin was beside her, his hand in its great leather gauntlet grasping her wrist like an iron band. And Ben, grinning malevolently, dismounted and stood to Boyo's head on her other side, while the third rider remained on his horse in the background.

"It seems we meet again," said Milord, twisting her hand until her wrist was forced up against her back.

"What do you—what is this—" sputtered Andrea. "I left the village as you ordered! Why—?"

Lord Justin had taken in the avid face of the innkeeper. "It is a pity you did not leave my horse, then," purred Milord. "And, I think, my purse also. Search him, Ben."

Grinning, Ben approached. Andrea knew she could not endure his hands fumbling at her body. She released her reins and pulled her purse out of her coat pocket with the hand Milord was not holding. "This is my own purse. As you can see, it is not yours—"

"Is it not? Then I am much mistaken, you young thief."

The innkeeper entered the conversation excitedly. "Did I not say so, myself? I knew the horse was too fine for such a oddly-dressed boy! Anyone with half an eye can see that the coat doesn't fit him—is it yours, your honor?"

Lord Justin shuddered elaborately. "Not mine, I am glad to say. I am Justin of Kyle, landlord."

The innkeeper was bowing almost to his knees. "Just this moment, before your lordship rode up, this barefaced wretch sought to pay me for a night's lodging with some of your lordship's gold!"

"Did he, indeed? Then you were a smart man not to touch it, lest you be held for receiving stolen goods."

White-faced, since the penalty for that could have been deportation or worse, the innkeeper backed away in a gabble of explanations and apologies. He was only too thankful to see the last of both thief and victims, and went into the inn, shutting the door behind him.

"Well?" asked Milord, smiling viciously into Andrea's face. "How is this for medieval justice?" He nodded to Ben, who caught her booted foot in his hands and secured a length of cord around her ankle. Then he passed the longer end under the horse's belly to the third man, now waiting to receive it, who tied it around Andrea's other ankle. Another cord was tied to Boyo's bridle, and then Ben mounted and fastened the other end of it to his saddle.

To Andrea's shocked gaze Lord Justin returned an icy smile. "I've seen you ride. I take no chances." He moved his horse over to jostle Boyo. "Ride out!"

Andrea found voice at last.

"What is the meaning of this farce? You know that is not your purse—and Boyo is mine! I demand—"

"You had better pipe down, you lying young devil! Be thankful I don't string you up out of hand. I'm taking you back to the Castle, where I intend to get to the bottom of your little conspiracy. If I tell you that your saddle has been found, and tied to it some very interesting items, you may understand that your imposture is over."

"My saddle?" faltered Andrea.

"Exactly so. It is unfortunate for you that you did not know about the strong undercurrent which washes the cliffs beneath Kyle Castle, and tosses things up on the beach in the next cove to the south." He stared at her, waiting her reply, but Andrea was too stunned to comment.

Milord laughed. "That's silenced you, has it? It only wanted your putting the blame on William—if that's his real name—to damn you in my eyes. At least you've got that much loyalty to the man who's tried to protect you!"

"Protect?" Andrea seemed unable to do more than repeat his words. He frowned at her.

"Yes. I've questioned him again. He claims it was he who wore the ghost costume the first time, and rode your horse, while you were dallying with Freda at the inn. Why he should seek to protect you I do not know, but I intend to find out. I shall also discover exactly who the both of you are, and what you had hoped to accomplish by your—activities in Kyle Village."

Lord Justin gave the office, and the little cavalcade moved back along the highroad toward Kyle. Andrea rode with drooping head, conscious of Ben glowering beside her, and the tall, broad-shouldered figure of Milord going ahead. After the exertions and excitements of the day, it seemed there was no more iron left in her backbone. She tried to straighten her shoulders when the party stopped at a tavern for hot beef and bread. She ate thankfully. She refused ale, and sat quietly while the rest quaffed theirs. In a few minutes they resumed their journey, with Milord still in the lead.

About midnight, Lord Justin fell back and took his place beside the drooping figure.

"Do you wish to get down and relieve yourself, or stretch your legs?"

If there had been even a hint of concern in Milord's voice, Andrea might have told him everything in that moment. But his tone was insultingly impersonal, as one tending to the needs of his cattle.

The girl's head came up. "No, I thank you." she said. There was no need to deepen her voice deliberately. It was so hoarse with strain and unhappiness that it came out a gruff little croak.

"Do not seek to win my pity by childish tricks," Lord Justin advised her cuttingly. "I know you now for what you are—a bare-faced liar, hiding God knows what depravity under a cloak of pious innocence."

Andrea made no reply. There seemed to be nothing to say. Perhaps when they reached the Castle, the charges against her would be made clear, and she could try to defend herself. Now she was too weary to speak, or think.

Chapter Fourteen

THE LITTLE CAVALCADE ARRIVED in Kyle Village just before dawn. They rode slowly through the sleeping street and on up the winding road through the forest to the castle. Andrea passed through the massive gates in the great wall half asleep, half fainting with weariness. Every bone ached; every muscle was stiff. Her flesh was bruised and sore.

They came to a halt before a flight of shallow steps leading up to great double doors of oak and iron. Ben untied the cord about Andrea's ankles, then reached up and jerked her arm. Dazed and stiff, Andrea was unable to save herself. She fell to the cobblestones of the courtyard. Perhaps her extreme exhaustion saved her from broken bones, for she was too limp to tense herself against the fall. Milord spoke sharply.

"Get some food and rest, Ben. Report to me in four hours. You too, Matt."

"Shouldn't I toss this young blaggard in a cell first, your lordship?"

"I need him alive and in his senses for questioning," Lord Justin answered with a grim smile. "You are a thought too eager to avenge yourself upon him." He bent down and pulled Andrea to her feet by one arm. "Walk, Bartholomew!"

Andrea stumbled after the tall figure into the lighted castle. Never afterward could she remember anything she saw on that first entry—there was a dazzle of lamps and candles, marble floors covered with soft rugs at intervals, and a sweet smell of potpourri. She came to her full senses when Milord held a small glass of brandy to her lips and forced her to drink. The pungent smell and taste of the liquor was a sharp restorative. Andrea focused and discovered herself to be in a large, well-appointed room lined with bookshelves and containing a huge fireplace. A fire had been newly kindled. Lord Justin went across to his desk and seated himself behind it. He waved Andrea to a chair before the desk.

"You may be seated during this first questioning," Milord said grimly. "Later, if your answers do not satisfy me, I have other methods which you will not find so comfortable."

"Milord," Andrea had to fight for her voice, "by your leave, may I be permitted to relieve myself and wash my face and hands?"

Lord Justin flashed her an irritated glance, then nodded and walked to the bellpull beside the fireplace. "There is a small water-closet under the stairway. I shall have you escorted there. You may have five minutes."

When the impassive footman appeared, Lord Justin gave his orders. Andrea followed the man gratefully. The small cabinet to which he led her was up-to-date and neatly appointed, and it was scrupulously clean. There was a commode, a hand basin on a stand and fresh towels laid out. The footman closed the door after her and waited outside. Following him back to the study a few minutes later, Andrea felt awake once more and better prepared to face the challenge of the coming confrontation.

"And now, if there is no further delaying action you can think of—" begin his lordship. He did not ask her to be seated this time.

"I would only ask you of what I am accused, Milord," answered the girl with desperate quiet. She had been in the saddle for twenty hours. She was by now frightened of Lord Justin and what he and his henchmen, especially Ben, might do to her. Beneath the great amber eyes dark brown smudges bore witness to her physical exhaustion. Still she contrived to keep her voice low and steady, and her golden head high.

Lord Justin regarded the white-faced boy before him with a scowl. Every fact he had been able to uncover seemed to prove the youth a liar and a malicious meddler at the least. Yet every instinct Milord possessed warred against this judgment. The huge eyes met his directly; the narrow shoulders were held gallantly straight at a cost that showed in the pale, strained face.

Milord rose and pulled away a cloth which covered a heap of objects on the floor. Andrea's eyes flashed to the pile. There was a saddle, once fine, now salt-stained and ruined. Tied to the stirrup was a sodden mass of dark grayish material which might once have been a dress. Beyond these unpleasant objects was Andrea's small trunk, gaping open. On top of the man's clothing rested her botany note book, and the torn-out sheet with her drawing of Kyle Castle which Milord had removed. The trumpery fobs were there, too, and, like a swan among geese, the topaz pendant . . . and the jeweled dagger of Count Wasylyk!

"Well?" asked Milord, softly. "Let us take first the saddle. It is yours, is it not?"

"Yes."

"Next, this dress. Do you tell me it belongs to William? He has claimed that it was he who rode your horse and wore the dress and disposed of them before he returned to the inn where you were disporting yourself with Freda. What have you to say to that, halfling?"

The girl did not know how to answer. Why should William lie, taking the blame? If she could only ask him before she tried to answer Milord! But it was unlikely Lord Justin would provide them an opportunity to make their stories agree. She straightened her shoulders. No more lies! She owed it to herself to say nothing or to speak the truth.

"I bought the dress and wore it on the first ride."

Lord Justin nodded. "I am glad for your sake that you have decided to tell the truth. Alan held the garment up to William; it would be impossible for him to get himself into it. Now, this botany notebook?"

"It is my own. I have kept it for several years, since I was a child in school."

"I accept that also. The larger part of it has not been written recently. Why the sketch of my home?"

"I was interested in the Castle. It is beautiful and a little frightening." Catching sight of his frown, she added, "I wondered a little if I might find a way to enter it."

"I suppose you will now tell me why you should wish to enter the Castle?"

"You may believe me or not," cried Andrea, desperately, "but I really hadn't any special plan to enter. I thought the single ride of the ghost would accomplish my purpose."

"Am I to hear now, at last, what your purpose was?" sneered Milord.

Andrea hung her head.

Lord Justin waited a moment, and when she did not reply, he picked up the topaz pendant and dangled it before Andrea's face. "This very interesting and valuable piece of jewelry—? Did you steal it, or was it a bribe?"

Andrea's head lifted proudly. "No, Milord. It was my mother's."

"Did she have eyes like yours?" Milord asked, almost idly.

"So I am told," gulped Andrea. "She died at my birth."

"What was your reason for engaging in this unpleasant charade?"

The girl could not think what to answer. She dared not claim to be Pola's sister, for his next act would probably be to strip her to make sure of her claim. She did not think she could bear to have her man's clothing removed by those big hands. She knew now that she had acted with criminal folly in entering upon this masquerade. Yet having done so, if she could only get herself out of Kyle without revealing her true name and sex, she might save something of self-respect. Andrea had a sick fear of the treatment a vagabond girl, already suspect of nameless crimes, might receive at the hands of Lord Justin and Ben.

When it was evident that she was reluctant to answer, Justin continued in a reasonable voice, "If you will tell me freely now what you were really doing in Kyle Village, why you pretended to be a ghost, and what you know of—my wife, I might be persuaded to change my intention of beating the truth out of you. As I have tried to do with William," he added grimly. "This is your last chance, boy. Believe me, for I play no more games, nor will I permit you to do so."

Andrea put a hand to her forehead. If she were not so tired! If she could have time to think!

Lord Justin seemed to read her expression.

"Now," he said implacably.

Andrea kept silent. What could she say? She swayed a little, but he did not ask her to sit down.

"You will not confess voluntarily? Then I must ask you further questions. Do not lie to me. That will bring its own extra punishment. First then, *what is your name?*"

It was hopeless! If she only knew what was best to be done! She did not believe this arrogant man had killed Pola, but how could she be sure? He had beaten William cruelly. She knew she was too naive to be a judge of men, yet his behavior in accusing her of the theft of Boyo and his purse, his abduction of her, these were surely not the actions of an innocent man of good will?

"I cannot tell you my name, Milord," she said wearily.

"It is not, in fact, Tad Bartholomew?"

"No."

Lord Justin slammed his fist on the desk. "You will address me in proper form, boy!"

It seemed a small point to arouse such anger. She would never understand men! "No, Lord Justin."

"Why did you come to Kyle?"

"I came seeking information, Milord."

"What information?"

"I wished to find out exactly how your—how Lady Justin died."

Lord Justin's eyes narrowed into icy slits. "Who employed you as a spy?"

Andrea drew a ragged breath. "I cannot tell you, Milord." She could not bear to meet the merciless gaze of those accusing eyes. There was a pause.

Then Lord Justin snapped, "You young fool, whom are you protecting? Don't you realize what a desperate coil you've gotten yourself into?"

"Yes, Milord, I do." Andrea tried to smile. It was a failure, more a grimace of pain. "I—I cannot tell you, sir. Oh, let me rest!"

"You'll rest when you've satisfied me on all counts," said Milord grimly. "This is your last chance to avoid painful interrogation, boy. Will you tell me what I wish to know?"

"I cannot," whispered Andrea.

Milord shrugged and walked over to the bell-pull. In a moment the footman appeared. "Send Ben and Alan to me at once."

"Yes, Milord."

The Master of Kyle stood looking into the fire until the door opened and the two men walked into the room. Ben stood behind Andrea's drooping figure.

"Take him down to the dungeon and leave him in a cell near William. Do not let them talk. I shall be down to conduct the questioning when I have eaten." His eyes rested on Ben's avid face. "Do nothing to either of them until I come."

"Yes, Milord." Ben caught Andrea's arm and pulled her from the room. After a searching look at his master, Alan followed.

Andrea was too tired to feel fear as she was half-led, half-jostled down the wide stone stairs. First there had been the massive wood door at one side of the enormous central hall of the castle. When Alan swung it open, a waft of sour, earthy air swept into the girl's face, reminding her more of the grave than of a prison. Huge flambeaux burned in iron cages against the walls. The wide stairway seemed to go down forever. At length, however, it straightened out into a room which had once been a guardroom, from the looks of the ancient furniture. Beyond this, through an archway, was the prison itself. A wide central corridor was flanked on one side by small cells, while on the other side rings of iron were driven into the stone wall at various heights. Some had chains depending from them. This was all that Andrea's horrified glance could make out before she was thrust forcefully into one of the dark, open cells. Of course she fell to her knees, but she got her hands out in time to break the fall against a thick layer of straw. The door clanged shut behind her, leaving her almost in the dark, since the flambeau opposite her cell had not been lighted.

Somehow nothing much seemed to matter. There was a thick curtain between her senses and the outer world. Andrea's crying need was to rest. She sought a comfortable position on the straw, and, pillowing her head on her bent arm, was asleep in a minute.

She was rudely awakened by a heavy boot nudging ungently at her side. She cried out and pulled herself to her knees. In the light of half a dozen torches, Milord was watching her through the open cell door. Alan, looking stern, stood at his shoulder, and Ben was pulling her up to her feet with a rough hand under her armpit.

"Bring him out," commanded Milord.

Andrea was thrust into the lighted corridor and brought to stand blinking in front of Lord Justin. The latter held a heavy riding glove in one hand. Andrea thought he was the most beautiful thing she had ever seen, with his big strong body and handsome face, and the gray eyes gleaming in the tanned face. She ventured a smile.

Lord Justin did not return it. "Who is your employer?"

Andrea said stupidly—for she was still dazed with the need to sleep, "M-m-my employer?"

Lord Justin struck her lightly on the face with his glove. The blow stung a little, but the shock of receiving any blow forced Andrea's eyes wide open.

"Who is your employer?" the question came relentlessly.

"I have no employer. It was my own idea to come," she managed to answer.

"Then who are you? What is your name?"

"I cannot tell you, Milord."

Again the glove struck, this time harder. Andrea put a hand up protectively against her cheek.

"Are you and William working together?"

"I had never met Mr. William until Applegate introduced us at The Stag," Andrea said.

"Why then should he seek to protect you?"

"I cannot tell, Milord. I do not know, truly!" she hurried to say, as Lord Justin's hand was raised again to strike her. "Should you not ask him for his reasons? I am not being impudent, merely logical," she explained hastily, as she saw his face darken.

He hesitated, considering. After a moment he asked, "Are you a spy for Sir Ormond Talon?"

"No, sir, I do not know Sir Ormond."

"Yet when I encountered you once in my wood, you said you were going to Talon House and had missed your way. Was that a lie?"

"No, Milord. I was going there, in the hope of picking up some information . . ."

Her eyes dropped under the contempt in his. He held out his hand slowly and Alan placed something in it. *It was Count Wasylyk's dagger!*

"Is this also something which belongs to your mother? Like the pendant? Or are you a thief as well as a liar?"

Andrea said nothing, but her huge eyes burned in her pale face.

"Can it be that these two very valuable objects were your pay for spying? Were you in the employ of Count Wasylyk, he who was my wife's father?"

Too late Andrea realized that she should have told this terrible man the truth when first he asked her. How much better to have owned her scheme openly than to have it dragged from her in this degrading manner! Yet—*toujours l'audace!* she reminded herself wryly, feeling how far she fell short of the Wasylyk courage. The girl straightened her shoulders, and faced the icy eyes steadily. "I was not employed by the count," said Andrea. A wave of faintness swept over her. Papa was dead, and by whose hand? Dared she challenge him? Dared she say, "Did you order him killed in the same ruthless manner that you abducted me?" She held her tongue. Too much was at stake. If she could satisfy him she was a foolish boy on some nonsensical mystery hunt . . .

Milord was speaking again. "Did you know my wife?"

Silence.

Milord struck Andrea again, unexpectedly and so hard that her head snapped back and she staggered. Ben was behind her. He steadied her and then thrust her back toward Milord.

"Why were you pretending to be her ghost?"

Andrea kept silent.

Lord Justin struck her again, this time so hard that she gasped and fell sideways. Through the haze of pain and misery, she heard Alan mutter something which Milord gave a harsh, brief answer. He signalled, and Ben hauled Andrea to her feet again.

"Now I shall tell you what I believe. I think you are some impecunious little poor relation of the Wasylyks, that you hatched a hare-brained scheme of vengeance, interfering in matters of which you could have no knowledge." His eyes were bright with fury; he seemed to be whipping himself up to a rage against the slender figure before him. "Is this the truth of your vicious little escapade?"

Andrea, appalled at how close he had come to the truth, could only stare, bemused, into that handsome contemptuous face. When he realized she did not mean to reply, he shrugged and his eyes hooded. "Put him back in the cell," Milord told Ben. "Leave a torch here and give him a jug of water. No food." After Ben had grasped her roughly by the arm and thrust her into the cell, Lord Justin addressed her again. "I had written to Oxford to ask about a student named Bartholomew, but since you admit this is a fictitious name, my enquiry has been useless. I intend to keep you here, on bread and water, until either you or William tells me what I wish to know. On the other hand, I may have you stripped and beaten until you talk. I'll think about it until tomorrow. Perhaps you had better think about it, too."

It was the longest twenty-four hours Andrea had ever spent. When the flambeau in the corridor burned out, another was put in its place, so there was always light. This was at first a comfort to the girl, and when she found a large pile of clean straw on which she could lie down in comfort, and discovered the dark hole in one corner of the cell which served as a privy, she was able to fall asleep, telling herself that she had only a few hours to hold to her courage, until Lord Justin would set her free.

But later, waking with a shiver of revulsion

as something ran over her foot, she knew she would have to come to terms with Lord Justin and tell him the truth. She could not be expected to share a cell with rats or whatever it was that wakened her. Nor could she be comfortable in a cell whose whole extent could be seen by any guard who happened to be in the corridor.

A dull bud of anger in her breast burst into warmth. Fine daughter of The Wasylyk she was, to talk of courage and prate of her daring boldness! Her behavior had disgraced her line! Pola would never have trembled and temporized! Her sister's contempt for her had been justified. Then her anger turned against her oppressor. What kind of a wretch was the master of Kyle, that he could throw people into his dungeons without—what was the English phrase?—due process of law? Was it for this that the barons had forced King John to sign the Magna Carta? As the hungry hours went on, her anger burned more fiercely and she finally picked up the empty water jug and hit it repeated against the bars.

There was a curse from the guardroom and then heavy steps pounding toward her cell. Ben thrust his sleep-drugged face against the bars and growled. "What the hell do you want? Whatever it is, you ain't to have it!"

"Tell your tyrant of a master that I wish to talk to him," Andrea said sharply.

"Are you a knock-in-the-cradle?" snarled Ben. "It's past midnight! You can wait to tell him whatever it is in the morning. And if you wake me again, you little scut, I'll come in there and thrash you."

"There are rats," said Andrea stiffly.

"They only go for the soft spots like your ears and eyeballs," mocked Ben, and went back to his cot in a better humor.

Andrea spent a very unquiet night.

Chapter Fifteen

IT WAS IMPOSSIBLE for Andrea to tell the time of day from her cell, since it had no window and opened onto a stone corridor. The only light was the uncertain one from the flambeau in its metal cage. She rose finally and tried to tidy her apparel, combed her hair with her fingers, and uptilted the water jug for the last few drops to slake her thirst. Then she stationed herself near the cell door, where she could get early warning of Lord Justin's approach.

It seemed a very long time to the hungry, thirsty girl before there was any sound save an occasional snore from the guardroom. She had leisure to wonder if Milord intended to leave her to molder away in this hideous place, and her thoughts went again to how differently Pola would have handled the situation. Finally she heard several sets of footsteps upon the great stone stairs, and a confused mumble of voices from the guardroom. Then there was a sudden brightness as several more torches were added to the dying flambeaux in the corridor. Andrea came to stand directly in front of the cell door, and in a minute Lord Justin's big figure was facing her through the bars.

He looked so clean and comfortable that her temper flared. How dared he make her so wretched while he enjoyed a soft bed and good hot food? She glared at him through the bars.

Lord Justin stared back at her coolly. "Ben tells me you had a change of mind during the night," he began. "Have you decided to tell me what I want to know?"

"I did intend to then," snapped Andrea. "I'm not so sure I want to oblige you now."

It was the wrong thing to say. Milord's lips tightened. He gestured to Ben. "Get him out of there and strip him. Then you can shackle him to the wall."

"What are you going to do?" faltered the girl.

"What I should have done at first. I shall whip you, to get you in the proper frame of mind, and then I shall ask you the questions once more," answered Milord grimly. "I have been patient with your childish obstinacy and insolence long enough."

Grinning, Ben had the door open and pursued Andrea into one corner of the cell, where she had hastily retreated. He took her arm in a grip of iron and hauled her out into the corridor. Then he put one great ham-like paw on her overcoat at the back, and stripping it down off her shoulders, threw it on the floor. Next he hooked his fingers into the rather grimy white linen shirt she wore.

The girl cried out. "Milord! I will answer you! Don't let him—"

"Too late," said his lordship grimly. "You had

your chance—by God, you had a dozen chances! I have told you I'm done with listening to your temporizing and lies!"

As he was speaking, Ben got a firm grip and yanked downward on the shirt. The girl's hands flew up to cover her breasts—still concealed under the heavy binding she put over them when she dressed herself.

"I am Pola's sister! I am Andrea Wasylyk!" she cried.

Ben pulled back as though his hand had been burned. Lord Justin was rigid, leaning forward a little and glaring at the slight, tense figure that confronted him in the flaring light. He stepped over and seized her face in one hand, not gently, and stared hard at her, his eyes like cold metal in his dark, furious face.

"You damned little fool! If this is true, you deserve to be whipped! What kind of wanton hoydens are you Wasylyk women?" His gesture releasing her face was almost like a blow. The girl staggered back toward the cell.

"Milord, I will tell you what you want to know if I may just be taken upstairs away from this horrible place and permitted to wash myself . . . and perhaps have a cup of water . . . ?" Andrea whispered.

Lord Justin gestured grimly for her to precede him. Humbly she slipped past his big figure and almost ran through the guardroom and up the stairs. About halfway up she missed her footing, and might have fallen had not a hard arm scooped her up and tossed her over a broad shoulder.

"Maladroit in action as in speech," Milord said with a sneer.

Andrea wanted to retort that it was hunger and fear and weariness that made her awkward, but she decided that Milord would probably retort—and correctly—that she had brought it all on herself by her poor judgment, so she remained silent under the taunt. Besides, since her head was dangling down Milord's back, that she had better hold her tongue until she was in a less vulnerable position.

At the top of the stone stairs Milord hesitated, and as though to assure himself of the truth of her claim, his big hand came up to run over her slender hips. He muttered an ugly word. He did not stop in the central hall, but proceeded up the grand stairway to the next floor, where rich carpets deadened the footfalls, and statuary alternated with vases of flowers in arched niches.

In a few minutes Lord Justin entered a door, and dropped Andrea onto a huge bed. She scrambled to a sitting position and looked around her with interest which could not be denied by her uneasiness.

Standing by the open door, dressed in the impeccable livery of Milord's factor stood Alan. He was frowning at his master.

"This hoyden says she is Andrea Wasylyk, sister of the Lady Pola," Lord Justin announced bitterly. "You will send up coffee and sandwiches and a decanter of brandy."

"Oh, thank you, Milord, but the coffee will be quite enough for me," began Andrea.

"The brandy is for me," said Lord Justin coldly. "I see I shall have need of it to get me through our approaching dialogue." His manner was so hostile that Andrea began to fear she had not at all solved the problem by making her confession, merely changed it.

"You will also send up hot water for a bath, and bring a robe and underclothing from—my wife's room." Lord Justin was staring with disfavor at Andrea's masculine clothing. "Your sister's things will probably hang on you, madam, but I cannot permit you to flaunt yourself before my servants in that shameless costume!"

Andrea got off the bed and stood facing him. The worst of it was that she knew he had a point. "I am aware, Milord," she began stiffly, "that my conduct may leave something to be desired—" then, meeting his fulminating glare, she amended that to, "is unforgivable, but there are circumstances which mitigate . . . that is, I shall explain . . ."

"I trust I may expect to hear about these mitigating circumstances sooner or later," said Milord with blighting sarcasm. "Had you had the decency to come here to me when first you arrived in Kyle Village—" he broke off, regarding the slender figure with smoldering anger. "Good God, Andrea, I don't know whether you are totally lacking in intelligence or totally devoid of proper delicacy! No well-born, gently-reared girl would go racketting about the countryside *in breeches,* putting up at low taverns in the company of thieves and hedgebirds—! No woman of proper feeling—"

"Enough, Milord!" said the girl wearily. "I am in sufficient trouble without you compounding it with these mealy-mouthed animadversions! Will you withhold your prudish strictures for just five minutes? I will tell you what I did and why I did it."

"Mealy-mouthed—! My God, I'd like to throttle you!" said Milord from between clenched teeth.

Andrea said calmly, "You speak so cruelly because you do not understand. I was brought from my school in Switzerland to London to be an attendant at my sister's wedding. I knew that they had never accepted me fully, my father and Pola, because I am the granddaughter of a plebeian who happened to make a great deal of money and so was considered—" she met Milord's searching gaze and recollected that such family matters could have no bearing on his questions. "Forgive me! All this is not germane to our discussion, and I shall pass on without further personal comment."

"Thank God for small mercies!" commented Milord, still from behind clenched teeth.

"I did not know why my sister chose to be married in London, rather than in our much handsomer palace in Warsaw; nor why I should be kept close during the two weeks before the wedding—"

"That is strange," agreed his lordship, "unless, of course, your sister feared competition—"

"Don't be idiotish," said Andrea rudely, because she thought his words a taunt. "What man, having seen Pola, would have a single glance or thought to spare for such a gangling, plain-faced beanpole as I?"

"She certainly concealed you from public view," said Milord, and his voice was appreciably less harsh. "I recall wondering what was beneath that long green veil—"

"I am sure the question did not disturb you for any length of time," Andrea retorted coldly. "There can have been no shorter wedding ceremony on record. You hardly waited to drink the toast to the bride, and certainly did not bother to address so much as a single word to your wife's sister."

"That rankled, did it?" observed Milord.

Andrea ignored this comment. "We wrote to my sister several times after you left London but received no reply. Knowing Pola, we hardly expected a voluminous correspondence, and my father refused to express concern. And then he was brought home to us—dying." The wide topaz eyes brooded. Milord found himself watching the expressive little face with interest. She looked a proper urchin now, but with dressing, and rest, and care, and love . . . He shut off that line of thought abruptly.

"Yes?" he prodded.

."Your letter informing us of Pola's death was not given to me until the next day. It was—it was . . ."

"I understand," said Milord, more gently than he had ever spoken to her.

The slim shoulders straightened. "My cousin, Stacia Wasylyk, whom you met at the wedding, was a great comfort to me. We were of the opinion that there was something dubious about the manner of my father's death. He had been struck down and trampled by his own horses in the street outside his club. The horses backed and reared just as he was mounting his curricle. The man who had been holding the horses disappeared and has not been found."

"Not surprising, if his ineptitude caused such a tragedy—" began Lord Justin. Then he paused and gave Andrea a challenging stare. "You suspected a *deliberate* attack?"

"Yes, I am afraid we did. You see, there was the business of keeping me veiled and guarded within doors until after the wedding. Oh, I thought I knew the reason—that Pola was afraid some of her new friends would take the mineowner's granddaughter in disgust—but there was something not natural about the behavior of my father and sister during those two weeks. As I recall it now, it seems evident to me that they feared something—or someone."

"Nonsense," protested Milord. "A schoolgirl's fancies!"

"On the contrary, Cousin Stacia told me she had felt the same, and had even charged my

181

father with it. He admitted to her that there had been a delicate situation in Warsaw—a suitor of Pola's who became a nuisance, he said—and they had come to London to be rid of his importunities."

"You believed a rejected suitor might have decided to kill your father and sister?" Lord Justin asked incredulously.

"We Poles are not so phlegmatic as you British," said Andrea with disdain. "It was to me a reinforcement of suspicion when the news came that very day that my sister had been mur—that Pola had died."

"So on no evidence whatever, you chose me as the villain of your Cheltenham tragedy?" sneered Milord.

"My father and sister were dead," said Andrea with forlorn dignity. "To me it was more than a—a Cheltenham tragedy."

Lord Justin bowed his head. "You are right, of course, and my remark was unforgivable. Pray continue."

"I felt that, as the last surviving member of the Wasylyk family, I had an obligation to seek out the manner of their death. Bow Street was cautiously interested, and promised to prosecute the search for the mysterious stranger, but since no one had marked his appearance, it was a hopeless venture. I, on the other hand, believed that I might learn something if I came to the place where my sister had died, and made discreet enquiries."

"*Discreet!*" Lord Justin raised his eyes to

heaven. "In male clothing, and staying unchaperoned at an inn? I wonder at your cousin Stacia!"

"She thought it might serve very well," protested Andrea. "And so it would have, if your precious village had been a normal one, and not a feudal fiefdom! And if you yourself had been a man of reason, or even of common courtesy!" flared Andrea.

"God give me strength!" Lord Justin's determination to deal gently with the girl was being gravely tested. "I shall try not to interrupt your narrative again, madam! Please go on."

"Well, where was I? Oh, yes! With your intolerably close-mouthed, servile vassals and mercenaries." She glared at him to see how this hit had scored, but he spiked her guns by smiling politely, although his face was a shade redder than usual.

Andrea went on, "I was unable to get even a hint of how my sister had come to her death. Since I got nowhere by asking question, I strolled or rode about the countryside looking for clues—"

"Obviously a footless pastime," Milord could not resist interjecting. Andrea ignored this poor-spirited comment. "I had decided to go to Talon House to make enquiries of Sir Ormond, when Mr. William informed me of the presence at the Kyle Arms of the Castanes, who waited upon your lordship to inform him that my father was dead and I myself was missing from the school in Switzerland to which I had supposedly returned."

"I knew that your father had been killed—I had it from Alan. But you seem to have picked up the bit of gossip about the Castanes' business rather quickly, for one who claims to have had no success in her own enquiries."

"I had that from Mr. William, who is apparently better at getting information than I." She hesitated. "I do hope you have released the poor man. He has really nothing to do with all this. I met him for the first time at The Stag."

"Then I wonder," mused his lordship with a sharp glance at Andrea, "why he has been so assiduous in protecting your secret. For of course he knew you were a woman?"

"Ye gods, no! He threatened to whip me!"

"There seems to have been more than one of us threatening you, child," said Lord Justin with a smile. "What was your response to Mr. William?"

"I said I would bite him to the bone if he tried it!" answered Andrea.

Lord Justin raised his eyebrows. "Then I wonder why he told lies to protect you."

"Protect me? He nearly got me a beating from Ben, saying that I had spent the night with his precious Freda! I cannot think why William would have told you such a falsehood."

"I find myself puzzled by William's behavior also," admitted Milord," since his protestations, had I accepted them, would have removed you from suspicion and probably caused me to release you and hold him, if the saddle had not been found. Of course, when that and the ghost's garment which did not fit William had been brought to me, you were placed right in the middle of things again."

"Can you tell me how my sister died, Lord Justin?"

There it was, the question which she had come so far to find an answer for. Lord Justin looked at her sternly.

"Not to wrap it up in clean linen, your sister rode her horse over the cliff one stormy night when she was running away from me to an assignation with another man. She left a note."

His carefully level voice was devoid of emphasis or emotion, yet Andrea sensed how bitterly the statement hurt his pride, both as a man and as the master of Kyle. She did not offer sympathy nor challenge his statement. Pola had indeed proved herself the kind of woman who is labeled hot-at-hand, and if she had stirred up enough trouble in Warsaw to make it necessary for her to go to London, there was little use in protesting Lord Justin's charge.

"Then her death was an accident," she began slowly.

"As I told you, in that letter you apparently did not heed."

"It is strange and dreadful," Andrea continued as though he had not spoken, "for her mother, Countess Nadja, died in exactly the same way, that is, by riding her horse over a cliff."

"That is strange and terrible," agreed Milord soberly.

"Yet she was a superb rider," Andrea said. "Papa insisted that both of us become masters."

"I have witnessed her skill and yours. She rode fearlessly, but you are the better rider."

Andrea sighed. "So it was an accident! And my father's death, too. Somehow I cannot quite believe it yet."

"Preferring to cast me in the role of murderer?" Milord asked grimly. "I can prove I was nowhere near London from the day of my wedding to the day of your father's death. Nor since."

"There are always agents who can be hired," Andrea suggested, considering the matter academically. She was deeply enjoying the conversation she was having with this man, for she had had few opportunities in her restricted life to converse with fascinating noblemen. Milord, however, appeared to resent her comment. He said icily, "Are you charging me with murder?"

"No," Andrea hesitated, "But I still believe that the deaths were not accidental."

"Have you shared any of this with William?"

"No. I thought it prudent to keep my own counsel—until you threatened to strip and beat me in your dungeon."

"You have acted like a fool," Milord said crisply, with a return of his former hostile manner. "Whatever has happened to you has been your own fault. You must try for more decorum when you return to your cousin's chaperonage in London."

Andrea, suddenly forlorn at the loss of the rapport which had been developing between them, felt that he had spoken with quite unnecessary harshness.

"When you have bathed and eaten," Milord was continuing in that cold voice, "you must go to bed. Tomorrow I shall have you driven to London in one of my coaches. I shall arrange for a sensible woman from the village to act as your companion until you are back in your own home." He raised a hand to arrest her objections. "No, do not argue with me. Allow me to know what is best in this situation. You have demonstrated that you have no idea how to go on in society. Let us hope that no hint of this escapade reaches the quizzes in London, lest your reputation be irreparably harmed." He sighed. "The devil is in it, there are no female servants in this house. I shall send for Applegate's wife to give you countenance tonight—"

But Andrea had reached her limit. Glaring at him in a fury, she snapped, "Spare me your pruderies, Milord! My honor has not been compromised by anything I have done to this moment, and I am sure your own reputation must be so secure that you can afford to house your dead wife's sister for one night without the tongues of fashionable fribbles wagging—should such persons ever hear of this—a most unlikely event! You may count upon it that I shall never boast of the event! I shall be forced to accept your hospitality tonight, I am afraid, but after tomorrow morning I shall pray that I may never need to look upon your face again!"

The force of this peroration was somewhat diminished by the fact that Andrea had no notion of what bedroom she was to occupy, and thus could not stalk out of Milord's room in high dudgeon. However Alan appeared as if upon cue and led her to a charming room in another part of the castle, where a cheerful fire burned briskly, and a steaming tub sat in front of it. Best of all, a table set with piles of delicious sandwiches, cakes and jellies flanked the fire on the other side, attracting Andrea's avid gaze. As soon as Alan bowed himself out, with a twinkling smile, Andrea fell upon this feast. When she had partially satisfied her hunger, she stripped herself thankfully of her man's clothing and sank into the blissful depths of the bath.

After a good soak, she began to feel human again, and to regret a little her angry response to Milord's final tirade. It occurred to Andrea that she had never felt so many different emotions about any other person—anger, fear, hatred, even some remorse, as her earlier suspicions had proven unfounded. If there was another, deeper, response, she would not acknowledge it, but got briskly out of the cooling water and rubbed herself dry with the lavender-scented towels. She snuffed the candles and got into the comfortable bed with a sigh of pure pleasure, watching the firelight reflecting on the lovely old furniture and the gleaming silver candelabra. Just as she was drifting off to sleep, she had a thought which should have relieved her anxieties very much. Surely she could not expect to form a close relationship with the husband or her dead sister? This thought left her strangely dissatisfied, for one whose professed wish it was never to set eyes upon his face again. She fell asleep at last, and was troubled by dreams she forgot when she awoke.

Chapter Sixteen

SHE WAS AROUSED next morning by a gentle tap and the entrance into her bedroom of a neatly-attired, pleasant-looking woman she had not seen before.

"I am Miss Burkett, sister of the village schoolmaster," said the lady. "I am to have the pleasure of traveling with you to London to rejoin your cousin, Mistress Wasylyk."

Andrea sat up hastily. "This is very kind in you, Miss Burkett! I shall dress at once. When do you wish to set out?"

"Lord Justin advises that we break our fast before we leave, and since it is such a lengthy journey, we must start without too much delay. Lord Justin has sent a courier ahead of us to bespeak rooms at the inns where we shall be resting each night, and we are to have *two* postilions to ride beside our carriage!" the good dame explained with pride.

"Lord Justin is too kind," said Andrea colorlessly. It seemed he was so anxious to get rid of her that he was marshalling all his resources to bustle her away as expeditiously as could be.

"Yes, he is, is he not?" agreed the affable Miss Burkett. "Every care! Every consideration for our comfort! Such distinguishing notice! But of course you are in some sort related to his lordship, are you not? The sister of his young wife! Such a great tragedy!" The thought of it overwhelmed Miss Burkett, and she relapsed into silence with a sigh.

Andrea got up hastily and dressed herself. Pola's underclothing was exquisite. Her modish traveling costume was a little too short and too wide for her, but by cinching it in at the waist, she was able to make a fairly tolerable appearance. The colors also were not just what she would have chosen, but she told herself sternly that no one who cared about her was going to see her in them. In the event, this proved truer than she had anticipated, since the two ladies breakfasted alone in the bright oriel which had been most tastefully transformed into a breakfast room with a charming view of the moat, now turned into a rose garden. In spite of her unaccountable chagrin at the absence of the master of Kyle, Andrea managed to make a good meal and so did Miss Burkett.

Considerably heartened, the ladies were escorted out to a magnificent carriage by Alan, very quiet and zealous for their comfort. As they bowled down the road away from the castle, Andrea looked back in spite of her firm resolve not to. In the bright morning light, the old gray walls were softened to pale gold, and the gardens and plantings of trees softened the harsh outlines of the ancient pile to a romantic prettiness.

Andrea sighed and wished she had thought to leave a note of thanks to Milord for his—belated!—hospitality. Still, it was no one's fault but her own that he had not known her real name and person, so she resolved to write the note at the first inn they stopped at. Feeling a little better, she made a praise-worthy attempt to engage her companion in conversation. The older lady advised her that she always had a short nap after every meal, and, commenting favorably upon the well-sprung comfort of Milord's carriage, she fell into a light doze, and began to snore.

Andrea shrugged and stared out of the window.

The first day's journey went very well. When they arrived at the inn at which it had been arranged they should spend the first night, this was found to be a hostelry of the first consequence.

"There will be no need to mistrust the sheets here," Miss Burkett announced with satisfaction. "And the dinner, too, I have no doubt, will be excellent."

This was proved to be true. The ladies ate with quiet pleasure, a fondness for good food being about the only taste they shared.

"It is indeed reassuring," said Miss Burkett at length, "to see a young lady of quality who is not afraid to enjoy her dinner. It seems to be an object with many of the female notables who come to Kyle Arms to trifle with each dish as though it were repulsive. The cook there has confessed to me, almost in tears, that to see each plate returned with the food uneaten fairly breaks her heart."

The cook at the George and Garter was put to no such pain. After this meal, even Andrea was willing to go up to her bed-chamber and get between the unexceptionable sheets for a good night's rest.

The next day's journey was uneventful. Miss Burkett proved to be a boring traveling companion, since the rocking motion imparted by Milord's well-sprung coach invariably lulled her to sleep within a quarter of an hour after entering it. Again Andrea watched the pleasant country slip past, and wished with all her unregenerate heart that Milord was her coachmate instead of the somnolent Miss Burkett. Lost in such fantasies, the hours passed fairly quickly.

The day after Andrea and her *dame de compagnie* left Kyle, its master was annoyed to discover himself irritable and badly out of sorts. Although his public image was one of cold arrogance, his servants always found him just and kind, unless he was angered by their failure to obey without question. His intimates found him courteous, and, upon occasion, very good company indeed. High sticklers like Mrs. Drummond-Burrell had no fault to find with the face Lord Justin presented to society, deeming his cool insolence and meticulous observance of correct form very much to their taste.

Such admirers would have looked askance at

Milord's behavior this day. He snapped at his valet, damned his groom, and used his whip on his horse. That high-spirited and intelligent beast, startled by this ill-usage, did his best to unseat Milord, thus exacerbating his temper even further. When Lord Justin strode in to partake of breakfast after his ride, the word was all over the Castle that his Nibs was in a rare taking.

Alan, who had known Milord since he was in short coats, was not prepared to put up with any nonsense from one whom he had often rescued from childish pranks. He joined Lord Justin at the table with such a quelling look that Milord finally broke into a reluctant grin.

"You've a Friday face on you, Alan," he commented.

"That's neither here nor there," said Alan. "I know what ails your lordship, if no one else does."

"Oh, you do, do you?" Milord had stopped smiling, and stared at his oldest friend with his mouth "set stubborn," as Alan had used to say. "Well, granted you may know, there's nothing much I or anyone else can do about it now. I married the girl's sister, the more fool I, and a fine bargain that turned out to be."

"They're as different as chalk and cheese," said Alan. "It is all pride and consequence," Alan uttered another of the apparent non-sequiturs which had driven Dominic Justin to laughter or teeth-grinding in his youth. "You'd best be after her at once," the factor concluded, sternly.

"You old idiot, how can I?" protested Milord, feeling like a lusty youth for the first time in years. "I've told you—"

"You've a horse," replied Alan, as though the practical details were all Milord was worried about, "that is, if you haven't lamed him with your bad-temper, and you know her itinerary, for you planned it yourself. 'Twas that gave me the inkling."

"I know I shouldn't ask this, but—what inkling about what?"

"Your care in providing for the lassie on her journey to London: providing a chaperone, the best inns, two postilions, your finest carriage. Och, it was no inkling but an avalanche!"

Milord appeared much struck by these facts. "Yes, I do seem to have been excessively protective, do I not? Especially for such a harum-scarum, rattling little hoyden! Traipsing about the countryside in boots and breeches!"

"She's got courage, the lassie. And ye never did favor a mincing, niminy-piminy miss."

Milord gave a reluctant grin. "I do seem to prefer wildcats to tabbies, do I not? Bowled out by two Wasylyk women in a row! And there's the rub, Alan. A man does not marry his wife's sister! No, let be! It is for the best."

"The little lass is honest and loyal, not like that devious sister of hers. She was a——," and Alan used a very rude word.

Milord's eyes sparkled. "As I recall, you once

washed my mouth out with soap for using that very word."

"Soap never hurt any man, and you are changing the subject, your lordship!" Alan's severe expression softened. "Best bring the little lassie back here, Milord. We'll never rest with her off in yon wicked city. That wench Freda says William quizzed her about Miss Andrea's route to London, when she left, how many attendants she had. I would dearly like to know what he's up to!"

"You think he may want to marry her? He did try to defend her."

Alan shook his head. "If not William, it'll sure be another bad man, for though she's comely and graceful as a doe, she hasn't a speck of worldly wisdom. And if she was right about the deaths, she's in danger. Bring her home, Milord."

"I have a bachelor establishment here, Alan, in case you've forgotten," said Lord Justin dryly.

"There's that cousin Stacia, the widowed lady, and there'd be the abigails. 'Twould be a situation of unimpeachable propriety."

"My God, Alan, here's a transformation! I thought you hated women as much as I did!"

"That's as may be," said Alan. "Depends upon the lady."

"You old dog!" Milord grinned. Feeling remarkably cheerful, he gave orders for a small case to be packed for travel, and his horse brought round.

"You'll take Ben?" Alan asked.

Milord grinned. "And have the lady flee from me on sight? No, if you won't come, I'll ride alone. Better not make too much stir until I see what comes of it."

"Your lordship may be right," said Alan so smugly that Milord broke into a chuckle, and with a remark about old humbugs, strode eagerly out to his horse.

As the ladies were settling down to another fine dinner in the private parlor Milord's courier had obtained for them, there was an interruption. The innkeeper entered and, begging their pardon effusively, informed them that a gentleman had requested the honor of waiting upon them when they had finished their meal.

"For I told him," explained their host, "that he might in no way be permitted to disturb the ladies before that."

Andrea's heart leaped. Could it be that Milord—?"

The innkeeper quickly disabused her. "The gentleman says his name is William."

"Impossible!" uttered Miss Burkett.

"But that's what he named himself," protested the bewildered host.

"Whatever his name, it would be quite ineligible for two females traveling alone to receive a gentleman chance-met at an inn. You will refuse us, Host, if you please. With all proper civilities, of course," she added kindly.

After the innkeeper left, Andrea tried to argue. Miss Burkett shook her head.

"I have my instructions from Lord Justin," she said impressively. "It would be not at all *comme il faut* for you to be meeting a man at an inn. *Comme il faut* is from the French tongue," she explained kindly, "and means correct or proper."

Rebelliously Andrea went up to her room immediately after dinner to prepare for the night. Perhaps Mr. William bore a message from Milord? No, that was unlikely. And really, she was forced to admit, considering that Lord Justin had had him beaten, and that he himself had displayed such venom against women, it was just as well that Miss Burkett took her responsibilities so seriously.

Andrea was undressed and trying to calm her mind with an improving tract loaned to her by her companion, when there came a scraping at her window. The girl knew at once who was asking for admittance, and she considered for a full minute the propriety of the move she was going to make. Curiosity, to put it no higher, drove her to find out what Mr. William so urgently desired to communicate. So, first checking the bolt on her bedroom door, she crept to the window and drew back the curtain. Mr. William peered in at her from his perch on a sturdy bough.

There was nothing ludicrous or boyish in Mr. William's attitude. Instead, Andrea thought him to be a determined, even a desperate man. Pausing only to throw about her the dressing gown Milord had provided from Pola's wardrobe, she opened the window and asked Mr. William quietly what he wanted of her.

"To get in off this damned perch," said William bitterly.

"Mrs. Burkett would say it was not at all *comme il faut*," argued Andrea. "That means—"

"I know what it means," snapped Mr. William. "Are you a complete idiot? I had not thought so."

Andrea stepped back and let him scramble silently into the room. "You must keep your voice down," she warned him. "I do not want a scandal."

"What you are going to get is your death, unless you start using your brain," said Mr. William. Andrea drew back. His eyes had a glitter in them which she had not seen before, and his face was set in a mask of rage.

"Do you—mean to kill me?"

"No, you moon-calf! Lord Justin does."

"I do not believe you," said Andrea. "He is sending me to London with every attention to my comfort, even a companion to protect my reputation—"

"He is sending you to your death in a place sufficiently removed from Kyle that no person could ever suspect his complicity," snarled William. "Tomorrow at the latest—I had feared it might be set for today, and have ridden hell-for-leather to try to save you! Tomorrow, I say, Milord's fine carriage—such a spectacular and easily identified vehicle!—will be stopped by 'highwaymen,' and most unfortunately, in the course of the robbery, or perhaps because of their disappointment at the meager takings, the hired ruffians will slaughter all of you out of hand!"

"This accusation is monstrous!" Andrea held her voice to a whisper with difficulty. "No one but a madman would arrange to kill six persons!"

Mr. William smiled widely. "No one but a madman would arrange to kill his wife of one month because she was betraying his ancient name."

"Mad?" whispered the girl. "Oh, no, I cannot believe it!"

"For your life's sake, it would be well that you did."

"Why do you care? Who are you?" asked the girl.

"I had thought you might have guessed, but perhaps the great Wasylyk family is as short on brains as it is long on charm," William sneered. "I am that man whom your precious Pola deceived to the top of his bent, then betrayed and abandoned in Warsaw. But she had to flee from Poland! She and that father of hers knew I would never let her go!"

*"You—*killed her?"

This horrified exclamation gave him pause. "of course I did not! I loved her—so help me, I still do! Her precious husband ran her off the cliff the night he discovered she had left him to go to a lover. But it wasn't Sir Ormond—I was the man she was going to meet! And now that you have shown him you are suspicious, he will silence you as effectively as he silenced your sister and your father!"

"My *father* murdered, too?"

"Surely you suspected something? That's why you came up here, isn't it?"

At her desolate nod, he said gruffly, "Get dressed. Pack a bag and we'll slip away. I have two horses tied nearby. We can be safely away before dawn."

"Miss Burkett and the servants! I cannot leave them to be murdered. We must tell them—"

"The hired rogues will let them go when they find you have escaped. It is you the trap was meant for! Hurry!"

"Go down and wait for me below," the girl ordered dully.

"What? Can you climb down the tree unaided, young Bart?"

"If you wish me to accompany you, you will go at once," Andrea whispered. Without another word, William disappeared through the window. Only the faintest of rustlings announced his descent.

Within ten minutes, Andrea snuffed the candles and tossed her small case out of the window. William, evidently on the watch, caught it before it hit the ground. Then the girl, not without awkwardness because of her dress, climbed her way down the tree to earth. William caught her as she dropped the last six feet. Without a word he led the way through the inn grounds to a small copse beside the highroad. There in the shadow two horses were tethered. The man bent to toss her into the saddle.

"I can ride as well as you," she rejected his assistance. "Look to your own animal."

They rode away in comparative silence, keeping to the soft earth at the side of the road until they were a good distance from the inn. Then William spurred his horse to a gallop, and Andrea's followed willingly enough. When they had ridden for half an hour, William drew up to let the horses rest.

"I think we are clear," he said in a gloating voice.

Andrea was repelled. "Is it so important to you to have thwarted Lord Justin clandestinely?" she challenged. "I would think a true Pole would wish to confront him openly."

"You are a fool, Andrea. Would you have me call for the Bow Street Runners?"

"You think they would not proceed against so important a man as Lord Dominic Justin? I have understood it to be otherwise in this country. But no, I had rather thought a Polish gentleman would choose a face-to-face encounter."

William was not paying attention to her. He was peering across the fields toward a large building that topped a little rise. "A barn, I think. It should furnish us with shelter and some hay to rest on before we resume our journey. I have food and wine in my saddlebags."

"I am not hungry," objected Andrea. "I think we should press on toward London."

"I, on the other hand, am both hungry and tired, having ridden all day and half the night to catch up with you and—rescue you."

In view of this statement, it seemed churlish not to accede to his request. Andrea led her horse through the hedge and followed her companion to the barn. It was indeed an excellent shelter, being airy but protected, and smelling of the piles of sweet hay. Mr. William pulled the great doors closed behind them, and engaged the leathern thong which served as a latch.

"I'll build a very small fire to give us light and warmth while we eat," William decided. "There's a pile of old fencing."

"Will not a fire be dangerous, with all this dry straw? And we must tend to our horses before we rest." Andrea had been carefully schooled by the Cossack officer.

"No, we'll be going on soon enough. I don't want to be caught by some gapeseed investigating the fire." William crouched down by his small blaze and took food from his saddlebag. While he ate, Andrea perched herself on a pile of hay and watched him. As the firelight strengthened, William's eyes were attracted to her figure in the modish traveling dress.

"So, 'Master Tad Bartholomew,' you're a woman now?" he said at length, and there was a jeering note in his voice. "Stand up and let me see you!"

Andrea ignored this. She was having second

thoughts about the wisdom of this flight by night. Surely if they had told the innkeeper the story, he would have secured weapons and extra guards for their carriage.

"Miss Andrea Wasylyk," William continued softly. "If you only knew how eagerly I have sought you—the last of the Wasylyks."

"You have sought—?"

"Yes. After I killed Pola, I went back to London to dispose of the count and you. It was easy to manage Count Vladi—too many years and too much brandy had slowed his responses. But I couldn't get at you. They'd kept you so close I didn't even know what you looked like. So I came back to Kyle, thinking the grieving sister-in-law would be welcomed in Milord's Castle. But there was no announcement of the arrival of Andrea Wasylyk. Instead, a silly young student came pottering about the village looking for botany specimens. The disguise was clever, even if your suspicions of Lord Justin were stupid . . ." He laughed.

Andrea was staring at him, unable or unwilling to accept the horrifying things he was saying. Her shocked brain was echoing, "He killed father . . . and Pola . . . he's *mad!*"

"If this is true, Mr. William—*why?*"

"It's not Mr. William, 'Bart.' I took that name so Pola would not be warned I was near her. I did not think the stupid English would suspect me. But Lord Justin, damn him, was not the weak dupe I thought him. After Pola's death, he confronted Sir Ormond. Talon was able to prove he had not met Pola on that fatal night. Then Justin began to investigate the manner of Pola's death. He knew what a Cossack she'd been. He just didn't believe she had fallen to her death." He chuckled. Andrea was sickened by the sound coming from 'Mr. William's' lips.

"Your precious Milord became suspicious of me after your little moonlight ride. He had me stripped to find out if I were a female—I, Baron Niklaus Trygda! And then he had me whipped, damn him! I'm going back to get him, after I've disposed of you. No man lays whip upon a Trygda with impunity."

Andrea was not yet afraid for herself. She could not believe that this man really meant to harm her. "Baron Trygda, please! You must tell me why you have killed my father and my sister, if indeed this is not a cruel joke, and you have really done so?"

"Never doubt it, 'Bart,' " smiled the baron. "I shall enjoy telling you the whole history— before I strangle you."

He peered at her in the flickering light, then threw more straw on the fire, and some lengths of the rotten fencing. "You're a very pretty little female, 'Bart.' Now why should you choose that name, I wonder."

"My grandfather was Tadeuz Bartolomeu," said Andrea.

"Ah, yes, the restorer of the Wasylyk fortunes! The carefully ignored restorer! How I used to make Pola rage, asking her which of her jewels the dirty money had bought!"

"*Why*, Baron Trygda? You must tell me!" cried Andrea.

"Of course I must, little Impatience!" He reached out a strong hand and took her throat in a light grasp. "Such a pretty, boyish girl! You fooled everyone very neatly. Clever as well as pretty—and still a virgin, I'll hazard? Pity to kill the little woman before she's ever lived! Had I better do something about that, do you think?"

"*Why did you kill Pola?*" Andrea pulled her head away from his slack grasp. "Oh, I do not think you did so! This is the stuff of nightmares!"

The baron smiled into her face—and Andrea knew he had spoken truth. "I killed her because she was my wife, and because she caused my sister's death—a woman so far above Pola that your sister was not fit to touch her sandals. Oh, yes, you stare at me, little 'Bart'! But your precious Pola lusted after me, and I would not have her without a ceremony. How she hated that!" he giggled. "To have to swear obedience! She demanded that we go through the mummery in some remote parish where we would be quite unknown, but she married me—your bigamous sister."

"Then she is not—?"

"She never was Lord Justin's wife. I had no time to ask her if she had confessed to him before I forced her off the cliff's edge! Ah, that was riding! I have never done better, nor had she! I drove out upon her as she galloped along the cliff path to an assignation with Sir Ormond. Be sure she knew me then—I hailed her by my pet love-name for her! She laughed, and shouted, 'You here, Nikki? Haven't had enough of me yet?' and the lightning flashed and the thunder roared and we . . . and we . . ." He seemed to recollect his audience, and continued more quietly, "We raced along the cliff path, our horses shoulder to shoulder, but I had the better position, and I forced her over." He shook his head admiringly. "She had high courage. She must have known what I intended to do."

"Was it because she had left you and married Dominic?" whispered the girl.

The baron clenched his fist. "There was only one end for her when she stole my sister's young husband and then boasted of it. My sister killed herself, and Count Vladi took his notorious daughter to England and got a husband for her. When I heard that, I knew Pola had never told Vladi of our marriage. I waited, because I had not yet decided whether to expose her to public infamy or to kill her. But of course, in the end, there was only one answer. I did not intend to let her go all over Europe cuckolding me, disgracing a name as old and honored as her own."

"Pola was your wife, and you killed her." Andrea's mind seemed numb. She did not seem able to feel grief or outrage. If Baron Trygda was telling the truth, then Pola had brought her own doom upon her, and upon her family, too. Andrea struggled to think clearly. Was

Stacia safe from this madman? Yes, she had married into the family, not been born into it. And then there was Lord Justin, whose ancient name and fine reputation had been jeopardized by Pola's corruption. It was imperative that he be told as soon as possible that the woman who had so disillusioned him was not, in truth, his wife. But to what purpose? Pola was dead, and it might be better to let her shame and her crimes die with her.

The girl turned to her horse. "I will leave you now, sir. I must get on to London and arrange to return to Poland."

Her companion's laugh grated harshly. "You little fool, do you think I could permit you to live after I have told you all this? Although anyone of Pola's blood disgusts me, I shall take you here in the straw before I strangle you. It may appease my sister's ghost—and it is a fitting punishment for one of your family. Come here!"

Andrea turned as though to obey. Her eyes were searching the fire-illumined interior of the barn for anything which could serve as a weapon, for she did not intend to submit to this murderer without a struggle.

She saw nothing which would do, and the baron was advancing around the fire toward her with a wide, mirthless grin upon his face. The *fire—!* Andrea bent and seized one end of a flaming board, and brandished it at him.

"I will hit you with this if you come a step closer."

The baron paused, evaluating her determination. Then an even more devilish grin split his face. "The very thing! Does not Mother Church advise us not to let a witch live? I shall burn you alive and thus end the Wasylyk curse!"

Andrea stood her ground, but he did not at once approach her. Running lightly to the doors, he unlatched the thong and threw them wide. Then he moved to the horses, and drove them out through the doorway with a blow and a cry. Then, still not coming near her, he picked up a bundle of hay and threw it on the fire. As Andrea backed away from the sudden blaze, he ran in and kicked the burning boards and sheaves away. In an instant, several piles of hay were alight and burning out of control. With a final phrase in Polish that sounded like a curse, the baron ran through the barn doors and pulled them closed behind him. Andrea followed as soon as she saw what he was doing, but she could not force the doors open. She looked frantically around for another exit through the increasing billows of smoke, but she could see no way to escape. The hay was flaming up all around her, the roof was beginning to smolder. Thick smoke was everywhere.

Andrea snatched up one of the billets of wood from the pile and began to hammer at a wall.

From outside there was a cry in Polish and the sound of a shot.

"Good God!" thought Andrea in despair. "He has killed himself and left me to burn!"

Chapter Seventeen

A FEW HOURS EARLIER, Lord Justin, riding his great stallion and dressed with casual elegance in skin-tight riding breeches and a fine black coat, pulled rein at the King's Inn, the second on the itinerary he had provided for the ladies. He dismounted, and while the groom led the horse around to the stable, Milord entered the inn and accepted the obsequious attentions of the host. Lord Justin announced his name and style, and the innkeeper was moved to express his gratitude for the honor done his humble hostelry.

"Miss Burkett and Miss Andrea have already retired, I presume?"

"Yes, indeed, your lordship, they being much fatigued by the exertions of their journey," confirmed the innkeeper. "Has your lordship dined? Let me offer your lordship a simple collation—"

"Since I have not yet dined, being eager to reach this inn and assure myself of the ladies' comfort, I will have whatever your kitchen can provide," answered Milord, not best pleased that he would have to wait another long night before seeing Andrea.

He did justice to the roast of beef, the boiled

country ham, two plump chickens and the fine brandy, obviously smuggled, with which the innkeeper regaled him. Then, still too restless to wish to go to bed, and desiring to work from his legs the stiffness acquired by twelve hours in the saddle, he decided to take a turn around the inn before retiring for the night.

During the course of this stroll, he observed a window gaping open above a tree which grew strategically close to the building. At this point, Milord felt such a remarkable strengthening of those apprehensions to which he had been prey during his journey that he immediately repaired to the taproom and ordered the innkeeper to send his wife up to Miss Andrea's chamber to reassure him of her safety. While the good lady, much alarmed, was on this errand, Lord Justin first ascertained that no horses were missing from the stable; then ordered that Miss Burkett not be disturbed; and, finally, announced, when Miss's absence was confirmed, that he would at once set out to overtake the abductor. The host having told him in detail of the importunate visitor named William, properly denied an audience by the ladies, Milord had no need to look further for the abductor's identity.

After half an hour of hard riding, Milord acknowledged a fear too powerful to be repressed. He had no idea where William had taken Andrea. Then the even more repulsive thought occurred to him that the girl might have gone willingly. Lord Justin, more seriously concerned than ever before in his life, was trying to decide what was the wisest course to take when his attention was caught by the sight of a barn burning brightly at the top of a rise just off the road. And riding toward the hedge was—Mr. William!

Andrea was battering despairingly upon the stout wall with her billet of wood, coughing and choking in the smoke-filled air, when from behind her in the region of the door, she heard a shout.

"Andrea! Where are you? Call out at once!"

Her throat was dry with fear and the smoke she had been forced to inhale, but the girl managed to get out a gasping cry and hammered more loudly with her stick.

"Here . . . beside the wall . . . I am here!"

Through the flames and smoke loomed a tall figure in white shirtsleeves. He caught sight of her, and, running toward her, scooped her up over his shoulder.

"I seem to be making a habit of carrying you around in this rather undignified position," came the voice of Lord Justin. "You really need someone to take charge of you." He threw his coat, singed by the fire, over her to protect her from the flames, and ran out of the barn. "Thank God he set fire to it! I had else ridden right past in my search for you."

He set her on her feet well away from the barn, and as he did so, the roof collapsed with a great roaring and fountaining of flames and sparks. Andrea clung to his big body, and Milord kept one arm around her to steady her against his chest.

"He is Baron Trygda," gasped the girl. "He told me he had murdered Pola and my father, and now he planned to kill me, to wipe out our family!"

"Hush, child, you must forget all that," Lord Justin advised gently. "I am going to take you back to Miss Burkett, and tell them you were abducted from your bedchamber by a madman who thought you were his sister. In that way, no scandal will attach itself to your experience."

The girl caught urgently at his arm. "But where is the baron? He is mad, truly! Didn't you hear me? I told you he admitted killing Pola and my father, and planned to kill you also—for having him whipped!"

"He has killed himself, child. I do not wish you to see his body. When I have you safely disposed at the inn, I shall lead some men back here to bury it. If indeed he was a double murderer, he realized when he saw me here that he had run his course. He fired at me, missed, and then turned his weapon on himself."

Trembling, Andrea permitted Lord Justin to help her mount the mare the baron had provided. Then with Milord riding the stallion and leading the baron's horse, they went slowly back to the inn. Andrea knew that she must tell him that he had never been truly married to Pola, but it did not seem to her that this was the proper time. If ever there would be a proper time! Was it not better to let a sleeping scandal lie? If she told him, would he think that she longed for a closer connection? She bent her head in anguish over the reins. For a closer connection with Lord Dominic Justin was exactly what she most ardently desired.

The host and half a dozen servants attended their arrival at the inn. Andrea learned that this was the second time Lord Justin had come there that night.

"For you may well imagine," he was saying now to his gape-mouthed auditors, "that a fortune so great as my sister-in-law's is a temptation to every sort of rogue. I had thought that four servants and a *dame de compagnie* would be enough to protect her until I could arrive to escort the party to London, but it seems I was mistaken."

His triumphant return with the poor young heiress was greeted with cheers. He was told that, according to his instructions, Miss Burkett had not been aroused.

"I doubt if you could have done so short of a trumpet blast," said the poor young heiress waspishly. Everyone who heard her sarcastic remark charitably attributed it to fright and exhaustion from her ordeal.

"It was wise of you to permit madam to rest," commented Lord Justin imperturbably. "There is really nothing she could have done to prevent the abduction. Now that all has been so satisfactorily resolved, I shall require an abigail to assist Miss Andrea to her room to see her safely into bed. And I think a cup of hot chocolate, Host, to soothe her nerves. I desire that the abigail remain in Miss Andrea's room all night. This abduction has been a strain upon her," Milord concluded with such a minatory look that the innkeeper immediately begged his pardon for the occurrence, and promised it would not happen again.

At this, Andrea's eyes met Milord's in such a delighted sharing of the joke that the girl was forced to turn away at once and follow the servingmaid up to her bedchamber. All looked exactly as it had done when she left it two hours earlier, but what a difference there was in the girl's feelings! She scarcely believed she would be able to close an eye, with so much to ponder over, so much to accept.

The little maid helped her deftly enough out of her ruined clothing and got her safely between the sheets, then ran downstairs to fetch the hot chocolate. Andrea kept her glance on the doorway, hoping against reason that Milord might come to talk to her. When the door opened again, it was the little maid with the steaming cup. Andrea was fast asleep! Shrugging, the maid drank the chocolate herself and settled down in the big chair for the night, after carefully locking the door and both the windows.

Chapter Eighteen

ANDREA WAS AWAKENED by the sound of gentle snores. At first she thought she was back in the coach with Miss Burkett. Then she saw the abigail, cap on one side of her head, asprawl in the big chair. Andrea got out of bed and opened the windows wide to let in the fresh sweetness of the morning air. The noise disturbed the maid, who roused herself sufficiently to ask, between gaping yawns, what she could do for Miss.

Andrea's only desire was to be with Milord, but she prudently refrained from mentioning this, and said instead that she would be very pleased to have a cup of chocolate and perhaps a slice of the new-baked bread whose aroma was wafting up so invitingly from below stairs. As the abigail was leaving, Andrea added, carefully casual, "You might find out if Lord Justin has breakfasted yet."

Andrea was washed and dressed in the most becoming of Pola's traveling costumes by the time the maid returned. It appeared that Milord had risen very early to accompany the local magistrate to the place where the abductor's body lay, his murderous pistol still clenched in his hand. Milord had, however, returned, and requested the honor of a conference with Miss Andrea at her convenience. Thus encouraged, Miss informed the maid that she would be pleased to meet with Lord Justin in the private parlor of the inn in a quarter of an hour. It would not do to appear too eager!

In point of fact, she was there in fourteen minutes, but had the felicity of finding Milord before her. He greeted her with uncommon civility. Indeed, he advanced upon her so enthusiastically that the young lady had hopes he might have the idea of an embrace in mind. But this, alas, was not borne out in the actuality. Milord contented himself with taking both her hands, conveniently outstretched for his grasp, and looking searchingly into her face. His voice, too, revealed more emotion than the arrogant nobleman was wont to display.

"Andrea, my dear child, I trust you have had a comfortable night?"

"Oh, yes, Milord," the girl said, scanning his beloved features as intently as he did hers. "I am so glad you came after me! I should else have been dead today, burned to a crisp!"

The muscles at the corners of Milord's beautiful mouth twitched, and he said, in quite a different voice, "You incorrigible child! But yes, I am delighted indeed that you are not burned to a crisp, and on such a promising morning, too! One would not want to have missed it!"

Andrea realized with dismay that she had broken for Milord the mood in which she might have placed hope of him discovering himself prey to the tenderer emotions. For surely the firm clasp of his hands, the intent glance, the deep warm voice, had meant more than just a conventional interest in a young woman one had rescued from death? She tried for a recover. "There is much I must tell you—one fact which is really essential for you to know—" She broke off as she saw his almost paternal smile.

"Then we must have a serious conversation as soon as we have eaten, must we not? Our host has a nuncheon ready for us, he informs me. May I escort you into the dining parlor?"

Andrea was forced to accede to this reasonable but rather prosaic program. She waited impatiently while Milord ate a large amount of food with maddening deliberation. Finally he acknowledged her disapproving glance with a chuckle.

"There is rather a lot of me to keep up, you know! I'll cry quits now if you like."

"It does seem rather important that we discuss Mr. William—I mean, the baron's—disclosures," she said reprovingly.

He followed her stiff little back into the private parlor, his eyes twinkling with amusement. Her first words, however, after she had made sure the door was closed, startled him out of his light-hearted mood.

"Baron Trygda informed me last night that he had married my sister Pola in a secret but legal church ceremony at some time previous to her marriage to you," she began.

"What?" Milord sat forward in his chair, staring at her incredulously. "You cannot be serious?"

"I am. I am sure you will be able to trace the records in one of the churches within a day's ride of Warsaw. The reason my father brought Pola to England was that the baron's sister committed suicide for—for a reason having to do with Pola, and since the baron was swearing vengeance, Father decided to get Pola quite away from his anger."

Milord was looking very stern indeed. "You are sure of your facts, Andrea? This sounds like wildest fantasy."

"Since the baron is dead, I cannot bring him to reinforce my story, but he told me what I have just related to you. As I suggested, you could commission an investigator to search for the church in the village where the marriage was performed. Or there may be other ways to prove the fact. Your man of law would know, I am sure."

Lord Justin was beginning to look very angry. "Do you tell me your father knew of this—this unforgivable hoax when he accepted my offer for your sister?"

"No, I am sure he did not. The baron said Pola insisted upon secrecy. No one knew, except of course the priest who performed the ceremony, and the minor official in the government offices who issued the license. My father would never have permitted you to go through a ceremony with Pola if he had known about her marriage to the baron!"

"Your sister has presented me with distasteful options! But I suppose it is better to be regarded as an unwitting partner to a bigamist than as a cuckold!"

This was not going at all as she had hoped, Andrea thought. She had been foolish beyond permission to imagine a nobleman of Lord Justin's pride and consequence could consider allying himself in any way with the sister of a woman who had so shamefully duped him.

"I see that we have been a great mortification to you, we Wasylyks," she said painfully. "Perhaps the best thing for you to do, if you do not need me to make statements or witness documents, or anything of that nature, is to send me at once to London, Milord. Stacia and I will set out for Poland as quickly as possible."

Startled out of his anger by this extremely reasonable suggestion, Lord Justin turned his gaze upon her face. It was a striking face, with its huge amber eyes shadowed by strain and unhappiness, and its sternly elegant features. Not beautiful, no, thought Milord, but by all the gods, *lovely!*

After a moment he said in a low voice, "Is that what you would wish to do, Andrea? To leave me and return to Poland?"

Of course not! her heart cried out silently, but only the strained look in her great topaz eyes gave witness to her sudden rush of feeling. "I would do whatever will benefit your lordship," she managed to say.

"You must call me Dominic," chided Milord, digressing in a most confusing manner. "Do I not call you Andrea?"

"What has that to say to anything?" the girl retorted with more heat than she was aware of. "You also call me 'my dear child,' and indeed I am not!"

"Not 'my dear'?" asked Milord, treacherously.

"Not a child!" Andrea cried.

"How old are you, Andrea?" Milord asked gently.

"I am—let me see—why, I am eighteen! My birthday was last week," the girl confided, smiling shyly. "I had forgot it in the excitement."

"My God, eighteen!" muttered Milord. "And do you know how old I am? I am thirty-five. Twice your age. When *you* are thirty-five, I shall be fifty-two. And an old man!"

Andrea was busy doing sums in her head. "And when I am forty, you will only be fifty-seven. Your age then will be less than a third greater than mine. I should be catching up to you all the time! By the time I am one hundred, you would be only one hundred and seventeen—we should be a fine pair of gossips together! My old nurse, Nonna, came from Georgia in the Caucasus mountains. She told me that many couples in her country reach the age of one hundred and fifty and still find themselves happily married—"

She broke off as Milord, shouting with laughter, caught her up in a delighted embrace.

"You little rogue! If you are expecting me to perform at one hundred and fifty—! Not that I might not be able to, with you, you little witch!" Laughter on his lips and in his eyes, he looked down into her face. Andrea was shaking with joyous disbelief.

Then Lord Justin's face sobered. "My very dear, it will not do, you know." He put her gently from him.

"You mean because I am an insipid miss?" Andrea whispered.

"Whatever gave you *that* idea?" grinned Milord.

"Mrs. Drummond-Burrell told me my sister pleased you because she was awake upon every suit, and an insipid miss would bore you to distraction in five minutes. It is true I do not yet know any card games, but if you cared to have me instructed—?" She looked at him with hope in her lovely eyes.

He chuckled reluctantly. "My infant, that was not what Mrs. Burrell meant by 'awake on every suit,'" he said with a sort of regretful tenderness which put Andrea at arm's length.

Andrea searched his face. Then a new light came into her eyes. "Ah! I think I see. Mrs. Burrell meant that Pola had been in love with many men, and knew best how to please you in that way. Well, I am sure that in London I could very soon come by tuition in *that*, as easily as in whist or piquet!"

In an instant Milord had seized her so tightly

in his arms that she could hardly breathe. He said, between his teeth, "If ever I hear you make such an outrageous suggestion again, I shall beat you!"

"Tied up to the shackles in your dungeon, Milord?" challenged the girl, strangely enough evidencing no distress at the severity of his embrace.

Milord was forced to smile guiltily. "Now, don't you ring a peal over me for that escapade!" he begged her. "Alan has already washed my head for me. He tells me that all that commotion in the wine cellars has soured some of the wine. The dungeons have been used only in the capacity of storage for a hundred years," he confessed. "I must admit I set the stage to frighten our Mr. William and a certain impudent youth who went by the name of Bartholomew."

"Wine cellars! You are changing the subject again, which is very silly of you when we are faced with a real dilemma," the girl said severely.

Milord, who had somehow forgotten to release her from his arms, smiled down lovingly into her face. "We are?" he repeated, rather foolishly for one of his acknowledged *nous*.

"We are. If you must have an experienced partner, and I am supremely ignorant, and you reject the idea of another man instructing me, then you, it seems, must be my teacher."

"The idea is not without its charm," admitted Milord, kissing the tip of her nose.

"That is," continued Andrea with really incredible daring, "if you think you are able—?"

Since this sally got exactly the response she had hoped for, Andrea was quite unable to continue the conversation for a considerable time. There were, however, such satisfactory compensations that she really did not regret the cutting off of dialogue.